What Kind Of Love Is This?

2

Captivating A Boss

Tina J

Copyright 2018

More Books by Tina J

A Thin Line Between Me & My Thug 1-2
I Got Luv for My Shawty 1-2
Kharis and Caleb: A Different kind of Love 1-2
Loving You is a Battle 1-3
Violet and the Connect 1-3
You Complete Me
Love Will Lead You Back
This Thing Called Love
Are We in This Together 1-3
Shawty Down to Ride For a Boss 1-3
When a Boss Falls in Love 1-3
Let Me Be The One 1-2
We Got That Forever Love
Ain't No Savage Like The One I got 1-2
A Queen & Hustla 1-2 (collab)
Thirsty for a Bad Boy 1-2
Hasaan and Serena: An Unforgettable Love 1-2
We Both End Up With Scars
Caught up Luvin a beast 1-3
A Street King & his Shawty 1-2
I Fell for the Wrong Bad Boy 1-2 (collab)
Addicted to Loving a Boss 1-3
All Eyes on the Crown 1-3
I Need that Gangsta Love 1-2 (collab)
Still Luvin' a Beast 1-2
Creepin' With The Plug 1-2
I Wanna Love You 1-2
Her Man, His Savage 1-2
When She's Bad, I'm Badder 1-3
Marco & Rakia 1-3
Feenin' for a Real One 1-3
A Kingpin's Dynasty 1-3
What Kind Of Love Is This?

Khloe

"This room is to die for?" I told Luna. Today was her birthday and she wanted to party in New York. I had no problem with it because we were away from the drama in Jersey.

"Hell yea." She came over to the window and looked down. People were everywhere and the lights made it so much prettier. People can say its not all that but when you look at the view from a certain point, its really beautiful.

"How's Raina?"

"She's good. Her and my mother got into already." Raina was released from the hospital two days ago and begged her father to stay with me. At first, he was against it because he couldn't protect her. Unfortunately, I offered him a room down the hall and he hopped right on it. So imagine all three of us in a house and my mother popping up when she wants. I give it to Raina though, she gave my mom a taste of her own medicine.

"And her pappy?" I had to smile because he was trying to talk to me and I'd go in my room or tell him he was being

4

rude because Raina and I were talking. He'd just walk away with his head down. I still love him, hell I'm still in love with him but I can't be with a man who's ashamed of who he loves.

I admit that in the beginning, it was supposed to be about the sex but like most women, we believe the lies, fall for the bullshit and somehow get caught up in the illusion of sexy man really wanting more. I learned my lesson, that's for sure.

"Not a damn thing." I unpacked my things and placed them in one of the drawers. We were only here the weekend but I always made myself at home.

"Yea ok. One horny night and guess who's going on a Risky ride?"

"I'm not gonna lie. A bitch do miss it. The way he takes his time and makes sure I get mine a few times before him, shows how much he appreciates my body. The long talks we used to have and the getaway plans he wanted to go on, really had me believing he was my man."

"Ugh, he was."

"Yea but only behind closed doors." She nodded and I changed the subject.

"And what about that psychopath you're dealing with?" She waved me off.

"Hell no bitch. Tell me." I plopped down on the sofa and waited for Luna to give me the details of Waleed's latest craziness.

"Nothing much."

"Ugh, what's nothing much because you'll say that and it really be a lot more to it." I told her.

"He keeps threatening to end my life if I sleep with someone else. You know, the normal that he's been doing. Oh and he's gonna knock my teeth out regardless for having a slick mouth and to make sure no man gets their dick sucked again." My stomach was hurting from laughing so hard. Those two are pure comedy and I always get a kick outta them. She sat next to me and laid her head on my shoulder.

"Do you know if we weren't big girls, we'd have the perfect men? Fine, rich and great in bed." She said and I had to agree.

"I know." I rested my head on the couch.

"You ever thought about going on a diet?" I asked and she looked at me.

"For the sake of love, I've thought about it. But then, I had to think about my own happiness."

"What you mean?" She made herself comfortable before answering.

"I'd be asking myself everyday if it's worth it. I mean we could lose weight, be the baddest bitches walking the planet and a nigga still cheat. Trump did it to his wife." I almost fell out of the couch from laughing at that crazy ass analogy.

"Bitch his wife ain't bad. She looks like a damn orange; plastic Barbie and I'm not talking the original Barbie. I'm talking about the ones in the dollar store. The low budget ones." She busted out laughing.

"But seriously, after hearing Risky tell that heffa he didn't sleep with fat girls I contemplated going back to my old ways." She looked at me.

I used to eat just to throw up and I fucked up my stomach lining really bad. Everything Raina was going through, I've been there and done that, which is why I can relate so well.

7

The kids constantly made fun of my weight at school too. It was so bad, I never attended my junior or senior prom. Had my dad not made me walk the stage for graduation. I wouldn't have done that either. I was fine with them sending my diploma in the mail.

And my mother is no better and thinks she's not bullying me because she's my mom. It was like I didn't know how to say no or even stand up for myself when it came to her. She knew it too and played off it. The sad part is, I read somewhere that people who are related to you and treat you like shit, feel the same as her. Luna never allowed it to go on too much in front of her and I think its why my mom and her butted heads all the time.

"I love him that much and wanted to do it just so he would be with me."

"Damn Khloe. I'm glad you didn't."

"I love food too much and if him or no other man can't get with these dimples in my legs, cellulite on my thighs and big arms, then fuck em."

"Shit, I'm on the same page. I ain't giving up food for no one and this stomach I got, tells me all the time when it's hungry." She said and bunched it up pretending, it was talking like the crazy girl in White Chicks did in the dressing room.

"Let's get ready." I patted her on the leg and went to get my ringing cell.

"Is everything ok?" I asked Risky.

"Yea. When you coming back? Between your mom and Raina, I don't know who I'm gonna kill first." I could hear how stressed he sounded.

"Why? What happened?" He started telling me how him and Raina were watching television in the living room and my mom stopped by. She went in the kitchen, made her coffee like normal, went back in the living room and changed the channel. Then she had the nerve to tell them, they had their own room with a TV in it. Luna and I were hysterical when he said Raina went in the kitchen, came out and threw a handful of marshmallow at her.

"I'll be home Sunday."

"Be careful out there Khloe."

9

"I am." He handed the phone to Raina and we sat there talking for over an hour. Once we finished, Luna and I got dressed and were ready to partake in the New York life.

****

"What a fucking weekend." I told Luna as we drove home.

I called Risky and let him know we'd be back around two and try not to kill anyone before I got there. He said Raina was still asleep and my mom wasn't there. He told me if he weren't there, he'd be at the funeral home because someone called in from the hospital asking to get a body. I still don't know how he did that shit.

"Yes bitch, yes. I hope you still have those phone numbers." I nodded my head. We bar hopped the first night, and last night we went to Club Lust. It was mad fun. The strippers were cool as hell and all the guys were buying us drinks and drinking with us. We both met a few guys and promised to stay in touch.

"You better hurry up and get it in before Oscar locks you down." She sucked her teeth."

"Did you tell Waleed about him?"

"I tried but he messed up so there was no need."

"I guess." I opened the car door and stepped out.

"Call me later."

"I will and tell Raina she still owes me a lasagna." I laughed because she told Luna she knew how to make it and it was the best ever. Of course, Luna challenged her and now she's waiting to taste it.

I used my key to open the door, placed my bags on the floor and called out for Raina. Risky's truck wasn't there so I knew he was gone. I went up the steps and knocked on the door. When she didn't answer, I opened it to check on her. She's become my daughter and I found myself even closer to her since the incident.

Her bed was unmade; however, she wasn't in it. I instantly started to panic. It's like my gut was telling something was wrong. I went room to room, looking for her. When I opened the bathroom door my eyes almost popped out my head.

"RAINA NOOOOOO!"

Luna

I dropped Khloe off and drove to my parents' place. I hadn't seen them since my dad smacked fire from my ass and twice at that. My mom called and cursed me out. She said, there's no reason I haven't been there and my dad is an asshole. If I know my mom, she went in on him and he probably has showered her with tons of gifts to get back in her good graces. That's just how he was when it came to my mom.

I pressed the gate and waited for security to open. Once it did, I drove to the back, parked and went inside. Both of them were in the kitchen being fresh with one another. I cleared my throat, put my things down and grabbed something to drink.

"It's about time you came over. Your father has a few things he wants to say to you." He came over to me and looked in my eyes.

"Don't ever talk slick to me again or I'll do more than smack you."

"Really?" I had my hands on my hips.

"Really? Now." He took a seat on one of the bar stools.

"Your sister has returned but she nowhere to be found." He said with a snarl on his face. When I say my father couldn't stand her, I meant it. If he could've killed her years ago, he would have.

"How is that when I keep running into her ugly ass?" I grabbed a soda out the fridge.

"If you're running into her, it's because she wants you to. I'm sad to report that whoever she's with, has shown her how to stay hidden."

"Ok." I didn't understand where he was going with it.

"Which means, I'm taking your mom away for a while and I want you to come." I tried to protest.

"Just until we find her. Plus, I found out some things about Oscar and his people over in Mexico and I'm not thrilled to say the least."

"What is he planning because I saw him a few days ago at the mall?"

"He's here?" Both of them asked.

"He was but I'm not sure if he's still around."

"Call him and ask where he is." He said.

"Daddy, what is going on?"

"Just do it." I pulled my phone out and dialed his number. I could hear a lot of commotion in the background and then he answered. I placed him on speaker so they could hear.

"What up fat girl?" My mom was livid.

"Fuck you. Where you at? I wanna discuss some things with you about this fake marriage."

"I'm around. Where you tryna meet?"

"We can meet at the soul food place downtown."

"Aight. Give me an hour." I hung up and asked my dad what's next.

"Meet him and leave the rest to me." He rushed out the room and left us standing there. My mom shrugged her shoulders and I glanced down at another threatening message from Waleed. He was really fucking crazy. I did get enjoyment out of it though.

I stayed and talked with my mom for a while and headed to the soul food place. My stomach growled as soon as

14

I pulled up. It was pretty packed but since the lady knew me she gave me a table in the back. I told her a guy would be looking for me when he came in and if she could point him in my direction. I ordered my food and was fucking it up when someone stood in front of my table, blocking my sunlight.

"Why are you here?" I asked and he snatched me up outta my chair.

"You know, I'm beginning to think you're strung out or something. I mean this threatening and stalking shit can't be good for a nigga who sleeps around."

"Your pussy is A fucking 1 Luna but don't get it twisted. There's plenty more bitches out there with some good shit in between their legs."

"Then go bother them." I waved him off and he snatched my wrist.

"I'm tired of playing these fucking games with you. Let's go Luna." He told me to grab my shit and meet him outside. He must be crazy if he thought for one second, I'd go with his looney ass.

"Wale, what you doing over here?" I heard her voice and he let go.

"Really? Get the fuck out my face."

"Let me explain Luna."

"Explain What Waleed? How you keep coming for me but you're out with another bitch? Or how about, me walking into your house where you know I have the key to and watching another woman ride your dick?" I saw his facial expression change. I guess he figured out why I was so mad.

"Or wait, how about finding out you slept with her more than that one night? Which one do you care to explain first?" I wiped my face with a napkin and started grabbing my things. My dad will have to be mad. I'll meet up with Oscar another day. I went to leave and he grabbed my arm as I walked out the door. Him and the bitch followed me.

"WHAT?" I snapped and his face turned to angry.

"Then you parading this bitch in my face. Was all of it a game to you?"

"Is what a game? Luna, you called me and I asked if you slept with someone else. You didn't answer and…"

"And you should've let me finish." He ran his hand down his face.

"But instead you fuck the one bitch in the world who has been tryna hurt me since forever."

"What you talking about?" He asked and the bitch stood there grinning.

"Are you serious right now?" Was he really pretending not to know who she was?

"Luna, this is.-" He attempted to speak but I stopped him.

"I know exactly who she is."

"Then who is she?" He had his arms folded, staring at me.

"My fucking sister." That stupid smirk disappeared from his face.

"Hold the fuck up."

"What's the matter Wale? You don't like fucking sisters?" Julie said. I shook my head and let the tears fall. Her face spoke volumes, even if her words didn't. She was happy to see how much hurt he instilled on me.

"You good ma?" Oscar said and I turned around to see him coming closer.

"Who the fuck are you?"

"This is what I was tryna explain to you Waleed."

"Ohhhhh please let me tell him." My sister jumped in front of Waleed and I tried to stop her but Oscar held me back.

"Oscar, this is Wale. Wale, this is Oscar; Luna's husband." I didn't even see him pull the gun out until it was already touching my forehead. If I thought Waleed was gonna kill me before. He was definitely about to kill me now.

Veronica

"Are you ok Veronica?" My mom asked when she walked in the living room. I had my own place but after Risky knocked my ass out at the hospital, I refused to stay there. My mom and I didn't have the best relationship but we at least had one.

"I'm fine."

"Have you been taking your medicine?"

"Yes ma."

"Are you sure?" She asked again and it only pissed me off.

"I said yes." I tried to walk away but she caught my arm.

"Have you told him yet?" I guess the look on my face answered the question for her.

"Honey, its been four years. You have to tell him."

"Exactly! Its been a long time. What would be the purpose now?"

"The purpose is because if you ever have a child together, he will make sure the same thing doesn't happen to the kid."

"Ma, he has a daughter." I kissed her cheek and hopped in the shower. I saw her mouth drop open and refused to stand there and answer more questions.

My mom had no clue Risky had a daughter and I planned on keeping it that way, until she badgered me about telling him. I kept her a secret because she'd probably be on my back to tell him sooner or even slip up and mention it herself. Who did she think she was anyway? I'ma grown woman and I don't have to tell anyone, anything I don't wanna.

When I got out, I wiped the steam off the mirror and checked my face out. Risky had both of my eyes black and blue and my ribs were bruised. Little does he know, I got a trick for his ass. Now that I'm better, it's time to put my plan in action. His precious fat girl won't know what hit her when I'm done with her.

"Veronica, I'm only going to ask this question once."
She was leaning on the door to my old bedroom.

"What?" I sat on the bed to put lotion on.

"Did you do anything to his daughter?"

"Anything like what?" I smirked and made sure to keep my head down so she wouldn't see. She stormed over to me and forcefully lifted my face.

"Don't play with me. Did you touch her? Anything inappropriate." I attempted to move my face but her grip was tight.

"No ma. The medication is working." She gave me a crazy look and let go.

"Well, does he know your real name?"

"Ma, you know he calls me Ronny. And why would I tell him my birth name when you had it changed after your nasty ass sister molested me?"

I'm not about to give you a long story because its not really anyone's business so here's a quick rundown of my life. For those of you who don't know, my real name is Bridget Smalls. A long time ago, my mom's sister molested me for a

21

few years. I told my mother over and over but she never believed me. My aunt went as far as taking my virginity because she was using a strap on to sex me, which broke my hymen and as she says, made me a woman. Unfortunately, this went on until I couldn't take it and tried to commit suicide a few times at that. I did the pills, slit wrists, tryna jump off a bridge but the cops caught me just in time. Mentally, I was fucked up and they placed me in an institution.

I was released a few months later on medication and basically have to attend the crazy people meetings for a long time. Not too long ago, I met a chick, befriended her and she had a six-year-old daughter who was pretty. The little girl loved me and her mom often left her alone with me so she could work or even go out with her boyfriend.

Long story short, I began to get turned on by the girl and started doing the same thing my aunt did to me. The girl never said anything and did cry a few times. However, I ignored her pleas and started doing it more. Her mom came home early and caught me. She literally tried to kill me and once the cops came, they locked me up for five years.

I was released seven years ago and placed as a sex offender and couldn't be anywhere near children. If I did, I would be in jail a lot longer. My mom knew this and had me get my name changed because moving to a new state, she didn't want anyone to find out my background. She told me, I needed a new start and the only way to get it, is a new identity. I agreed and I was fine until meeting Risky.

He was everything I wanted in a man and his daughter was the cutest thing. She was chunky but nit fat, the way I made her feel. Anyway, after the first year of being together, those sexual feelings came and I started doing the same to her. The difference is she was older and could handle more. That girl was my soulmate and when she got older, I was gonna make sure we were together.

"I can't apologize enough Veronica but you can't go around doing it to others." She headed to the door.

"You have to tell him." I closed the door on her and sat on my bed. If I told Risky, he'd bury me. My mom is crazy as hell for even thinking, I'd do that.

****

After putting my clothes on, and eating the food my mom made, I went to my usual spot and waited. It was gonna take a while for him to leave and hopefully she'd remain in the house.

As I waited, it only angered me more to know he rested here for the last two days. He had his own place and yet; here he is under this fat bitch. What could she have done for him, I couldn't? Her pussy probably stinks because she's so big and her legs rub together. You know they say fat people have those black things in between their legs from rubbing so much. Yuk, how could he leave someone like me, for her?

Anyway, after sitting for three hours, Risky finally emerged from the house alone. I sat there for another twenty minutes to make sure he didn't return before making my way to the house. I walked to the door and couldn't wait to see how shocked she'd be to see me. Surprisingly, after knocking someone else answered.

"Hi. I'm looking for Raina." The woman stood there and looked me up and down.

"Who the fuck are you?" I snickered at her ignorance. This is the same woman who was here when I came to get Risky from here before. I guess, she didn't remember me and I'm not going to remind her.

"I'm Risky's, I mean Ryan's sister. Is my niece Raina here?"

"Does he know you're here?" She had her arms folded.

"Yes. I just hung up with him and he told me you'd be here. Your Khloe's mom, right?"

"Yea." She said and still didn't move.

"Can I see my niece or not?"

"I guess so. You seem to know about them being here, so you must've spoken to him." She stepped aside.

"She's upstairs." Her hand pointed up the steps and I listened to her tell me the door she was in, is on the right at the end of the hall.

"Thanks. She's gonna be so happy to see me."

"Yea. Yea." She closed the door, sat down on the couch and started watching television. I glanced around and the house was set up nice.

Once I got to the door and opened it, you could hear what sounded like a shower running. It only excited me more to see Raina naked and boy did I ever. I saw her through the glass bending over to pick up the soap she dropped. I slid the glass back slowly and by the time she noticed, it was too late. I yanked her head back, threw my tongue down her throat and it was on from there. I must say, I had a good time in there with my girl.

"That pussy stays wet for me." I buttoned my jeans up and heard the bathroom door open.

"What are you doing and Raina why are you crying?" Khloe's mom asked suspiciously.

"Just finishing up here."

"She just raped me." Raina yelled out. How could I rape her? There's no strap on here and I damn sure don't have a guy with me. I walked out the room and headed to the stairs.

"What?" Khloe's mom asked and when Raina repeated it, I felt a hard punch to my face. This woman dazed the fuck outta me.

26

"Bitch!" I shouted and started throwing punches that weren't doing a damn thing to her big ass. I got loose and ran in another room to try and get my strength. This big bitch was giving me the business. Unfortunately, she came in and we started fighting again. Lucky for me the bitch tripped and I got on top. I kept hitting until it seemed like she wasn't breathing. I stood, kicked her repeatedly in the stomach and stomped on her face. By the time I finished, she looked like the damn elephant man. Raina ran out the room with me right behind her. I caught her before she made it to the steps, grabbed her hair and drug her in another room.

"Since you wanna tell motherfuckers I raped you, I think its time for you to die."

"No, please." I kept a tight grip on her hair, snatched the belt off my jeans and went in the other bathroom.

"GET OFF ME!" Her screaming fell on deaf ears. I punched her a few times in her stomach and stood her on the tub.

"Please stop." I tied the belt around the shower rod and her neck, as tight as I could and was about to watch her die. If

27

she didn't wanna be my girl, she damn sure wasn't gonna be anyone else's.

"RAINA!" Someone shouted and I panicked. Pushing her off the edge of the tub, I ran out the bathroom and in a closet. Once the person screamed, it meant she found Raina or her mother and it gave me time to escape. I hauled ass down the steps, out the back door and to my car. Let's see how Risky likes that. Khloe's up next.

Khloe

"Raina what are you doing?" I grabbed her just as she slipped off the tub. The way her body began to shake made me think I was too late.

I unwrapped the belt from her neck and fell to the ground with her. She looked up at me and started crying hysterical. I didn't move and sat there with her for what seemed like forever. I had to give her time to calm down. I also wanted to know why she felt this was necessary, even after everything she recently went through. Seeing the belt around her neck on the shower curtain rod, brought back a lot of memories.

"I don't wanna die Ms. K but somehow she keeps finding me. Why won't she leave me alone?" I moved her back and stared at her. I had no idea who she was speaking of because I know Veronica didn't find her here or did she?

"Tell me exactly what happened."

29

"Khloe, where y'all at?" I heard Ryan yelling and Raina's body tensed up.

"Raina there's no way I can keep this from him."

"Please."

"Please what? And why y'all on the floor." He stared intently at his daughter and she broke down again.

"Ryan, I need you to remain calm." I pointed to the toilet and asked him to sit down. At first, he protested until I gave him a look.

"Raina, do you wanna tell him." She hid her face in my arm.

"I came home and she had this belt wrapped around her neck and.-"

"RAINA!"

"I'm sorry daddy. She keeps finding me and.-"

"Who keeps finding you and I left you with Khloe's mom?"

"Huh?" Now I was dumbfounded because my mother's car wasn't in the driveway.

"I would never leave her alone. Your mom promised she'd be here."

I stood and went looking around for my mother. I called out to her and tried to get in the room she had over here but never stayed in. The door was locked so I asked Ryan to kick it open. My mother never locked doors. I can't tell you how many times I walked in on her in the bathroom. After he kicked it, I found her on the floor looking as if she were dead.

"Oh my God!" I kneeled down next to her and asked Ryan to call 911. My mother's face was mangled like someone beat her with a bat or something. Blood was everywhere and a few teeth were on the floor.

"No, no, no." Raina shouted and when I turned around, she had tears falling down her face.

"FUCK! Who was here Raina? Who did this?" I had to stand and run over to Ryan because he was shaking her.

"Ryan, not right now. Let me get my mom to the hospital and we'll talk there. Raina go put a jacket or something on to cover your neck and meet me downstairs. You will no longer be outta my sight." She stood there frozen with fear because her father was staring at me. I wasn't tryna overstep but when Ryan and I aren't around her, someone keeps attacking her so it is, what it is at this point.

"GO RAINA!" She ran out and I went back to check on my mom.

"Ryan grab me a towel please. I need to put pressure on this gash in the back of her head." He did like I asked and handed it to me. A few minutes later, I heard the sirens and asked him to direct them up.

"Ms. K are they going to make me stay at the hospital again?" I pulled her in the corner as the EMT's began putting my mom on a stretcher.

"Now you listen to me." I made her stare in my eyes.

"No one is taking you anywhere. Do you understand?"

"But..."

"But nothing. Get in the car with your father and I'll see you at the hospital." She nodded.

"Raina?" She turned to look at me.

"I don't care if your body starts to overheat in that hoodie you put on. Do not! And I mean do not, take it off." I looked at Ryan and he had a confused look on his face too. Knowing him, he never paid attention to the marks on her neck.

"We'll discuss everything later. Right now, I have to check on my mother and I feel at ease because she's with you. I'll see you soon." I kissed Raina on the forehead and him on the cheek. I wanted to do more but we're not a couple and I'm not tryna give him false hope or myself for that matter.

I hopped in the back of the ambulance and dialed my father's number. They haven't been living together in months but they're still very much together. Once I gave him the information, he said he'll meet me there. I called Luna but she didn't answer. How could all of this happen in a matter of hours? I spoke to them this morning and everything was fine. I guess it's true when they say things could happen in the blink of an eye.

****

The ambulance backed into the emergency room and two nurses were standing there with a doctor. They took my mom in and I saw Raina and Ryan getting out the car. She came running over to me as I watched her dad, waiting for mine to get out. Raina took my hand in hers and led me inside. The doctor told us to have a seat in the waiting room and he'll come out as soon as she's checked over. Who knows how long that'll be.

"How you feeling K?" Ryan asked and put my feet on his lap.

"Really, I don't know how to feel." He took my shoes off and started rubbing my feet.

"What you mean?"

"I come home and catch Raina just in time from almost taking her life again." I whispered because she was sitting next to my father and I didn't want him to hear. Not that he'd say anything but that's her business to tell.

"Then my mom is brutally beaten and not by me." I gave him a fake smile and he laughed.

"And last but not least, the man I'm in love with is rubbing my feet and showing affection to a fat bitch he said he'd never fuck." He stopped and stared at me.

"K?"

"No, I get it Ryan. You've gone your entire life having bad bitches by your side. Then I come along, give you some banging ass sex." He sucked his teeth.

"And instead of embracing what we could've had, you tried to hide me to keep people from knowing. I really thought you were different than these other guys out here."

"K, I'm in.-"

"Ms. Banks." The doctor called out before he could finish. I removed my feet, slid my shoes on and stood with my father.

"Please have a seat." He directed us to sit back down and I felt Ryan behind me. Sad to say, feeling him breathe on my neck made the hairs on it stand.

"I'll make love to you later K so stop getting turned on." He whispered and I wanted to smack him. I folded my arms and listened to the doctor.

"Your mom, your wife, suffered a fractured skull, nose and jaw. In which we had to put back in place and wire her mouth. She had some bruised ribs and a gash on her head. We gave her five butterfly stitches and two of her fingers were broken, as well." I had my hands covering my mouth and I could see my dad crying. No matter how rude, ignorant and fucked up as a mother she was, she didn't deserve this.

"It's my fault. This is all my fault. She was tryna protect me and.-" We all turned to look at her.

"Take her out Ryan."

"Ms. K. I'm so sorry. Please don't hate me."

"Ryan please take her outta here." I needed her gone. I couldn't take her revealing anything and she end up in the hospital longer. My dad glanced at me and I told him I'd explain later.

The doctor told us my mom would be in ICU for a couple days and due to the trauma, she may experience memory loss. He shook both of our hands and took my dad up to the floor to see her. I told him I'd be up after checking on Raina. He kissed my cheek and I walked out to the car where they were.

"Is she ok?" Ryan caught me before I could open the door.

"Yea. She's going to be here for a few weeks. Ryan, I know it's asking a lot but can you have someone here to watch over her? Or can you call the police station and ask them how I go about doing it?" He stood me in front of him and hugged me. It felt so good to be in his arms and out in the open at that.

"It's handled." I looked up at him and he wiped my tears.

"You two ready to tell me what's going on?" He gestured to Raina in the car with his eyes.

"Your ex, is the reason all of this is happening to her."

"I know she had her throwing up and tryna lose weight. I've kept her away from Raina but she found her at Lamar's." It was at this very moment, I knew he had no clue what was really going on. Raina never told him like she promised, she would. I stood there staring at him in silence. When he finds out someone is touching his daughter, it's really going to break him.

"Khloe if I hadn't told you before, I wanna thank you for being there for my daughter. I know we aren't a couple yet but you still took her under your wing and are protecting her as much as you can."

"Yet?" What the hell did he mean by that?

"Is that all you heard?"

"No but you don't have to thank me. Shit, I'm happy she confided in me because it could've been much worse. I mean it's a lot and thankfully we've been tryna keep her grounded but something about your ex is triggering these suicidal actions."

"I'm gonna find out right now."

"Not yet Ryan. Let's talk about this later." If she hadn't told him yet, its best not to do it here.

"K, I meant what I said about you being my woman." I rolled my eyes and he lifted my face to look at him.

"I messed up real bad, I know. It's gonna take me doing something extra special to get you to forgive me and I'm gonna go the distance because I'm in love with you too." I just busted out crying.

"Daddy, what did you say to her? Ms. K are you ok?" She hopped out the car and hugged me.

"I'm fine Raina. Your dad said something that I never thought I'd hear coming from him but I'm good."

"Was it bad?"

"No it wasn't." I looked and he had a big smile on his face.

"How about daddy takes you home and I'll be by tomorrow to pick you up? We'll have a girl's day and discuss what happened today."

"Ok. Daddy I don't wanna go to our old house or Ms. K's. Can we go to grandmas? It's the only place she hasn't found me."

"I think that's a great idea and when I stay home, we can go to my fathers because she'll never find you there." Ryan gave me a look and I was scared to ask.

Risky

"Ummm, the house your dad lives in used to be Veronica's." She folded her arms.

"I didn't know your dad was gonna purchase it. Even though he did, I damn sure didn't know you would have a nigga lost in love and shit." She started laughing.

"Anyway, she used to live there and I doubt she'll return. However, I do have my own house."

"Yea but she's been there and we want her to feel safe." I was confused as hell.

"What do you mean safe? I know Ronny has been forcing her to do dumb shit but she's not putting hands on her so why is she scared of her?"

"Ryan, I'm gonna tell you something and I need you to remain calm. If you flip out, you'll scare her and that's the last thing she needs." She looked at Raina who seemed nervous.

"WHAT?" I snapped by accident.

"Never mind. You're already getting upset and.-"

"Tell me K before I get angrier."

"Daddy, she won't tell you because I asked her not to. You're being mean and she doesn't know everything." Raina put her head down and Khloe started walking away.

"Come on." I took Raina's hand because I'll be damned if I leave her alone and she tries something or someone gets her.

"Khloe Banks!" She stopped.

"What?"

"Damn you're sexy when you get upset." She snacked my arm.

"Are you tryna mack with Ms. K because she doesn't like light skin men." Raina made both of us laugh.

"Oh no." Now it was my turn to fold my arms and stare down on her. I could see her blushing.

"Raina has a meeting tomorrow with her therapist. This is the first one since leaving the hospital. Can you make it?" I asked.

"Of course. Give me the information and I'll be there."

41

"And you'll be riding my dick too. Talking about you don't like light skin men. I can't tell." I whispered and her face turned brighter.

"Talk to you later Raina and make sure your dad feeds you well."

"He's taking me to the diner."

"Sounds good. Let me go check on my mom." She kissed Raina on the cheek and tried to do the same with me. I turned my head and caught her lips.

"Taste just like I remember."

"You make me sick."

"Don't worry. You'll be sick soon enough."

"What does that mean?"

"It means I'm gonna keep planting seeds in you until you're pregnant." Her mouth dropped and I winked as I walked away. Yup, she'll be carrying my kid soon enough.

****

"How's everything?" My mom asked when we came from the therapist. Khloe couldn't make it because they were sending her mom for a bunch of test and her dad wanted to go

42

home and change. I did take Raina up there and let her stay after the meeting.

I promised Khloe if I had things to do, she wouldn't be alone. Plus, she wanted her there anyway. I guess Khloe was her protector and I appreciated the hell outta her for it. I always thought Veronica would be a good step mom to my daughter but after hearing the things she had Raina doing there's no way. Bad enough, I continued fucking her. Not anymore though. She's on my most wanted list.

Raina didn't say much at the meeting and the therapist understood. She did ask for Khloe to attend and we promised to get her there. It's unfortunate that I'm gonna have to kill my ex but she asked for it. I don't know why, but it seems as if she's done more to my daughter then what I'm hearing. I tried to get it outta Raina but she wants to wait for Khloe to be around to tell me. It makes her think she'll be able to keep me calm. I hate to tell her but if it's bad, no one will be able to relax me.

"It's ok. Raina, slept in the bed with me." I told her and grabbed an apple out the fruit bowl on the dining room table.

"Why is that?"

"After everything that took place, she doesn't wanna be alone."

"I don't blame her. How is Khloe's mom?"

"Still asleep and they're running more tests on her."

"And how's Khloe?" She asked and smirked.

"What you mean?"

"Boy anyone on the outside looking in, can tell how much you love that woman." I sucked my teeth.

"She's good for you son."

"Ma, I've never had a big girl and what if people make fun of Raina for having a big step mom? I don't want her doing this shit again."

"I should smack you for even saying some dumb mess like that."

"I'm serious."

"And so am I. Who cares if she's bigger than most women? Ryan she was there for you when Raina tried to commit suicide. Hell, she visited her every day in the hospital and allowed her to stay in her home, with you included. Even if you weren't with her before this stuff with Raina, she's a great role model for my granddaughter."

"I know." I sat down and looked at my phone. It was a photo from Raina. Her and Khloe were in the cafeteria getting food and the two of them had the biggest smile on their face. I showed it to my mom.

"Son, don't let a good woman slip away because you're ashamed of what the streets may say. Look at Waleed. His woman is chunky, as he calls her and he takes her everywhere and no one has a problem with it. Of course, if they do he'll handle it in his rude way." I listened to her lecture me on showing off Khloe and she's right. If I love her, who cares what others think? Plus, she cooks, cleans, has her own everything and fucks the shit outta me. What else would I need?

"I gotta figure out a way to make it right."

"You damn sure do. Khloe doesn't seem like the type that'll let you walk all over her. You're gonna have to do something very special to win her over. And I'm not talking about diamonds or anything like that."

"I don't know what to do."

"Look online but whatever it is, make sure it comes from the heart. Trust me, she'll appreciate it so much more."

"You think?"

"I know she will. But afterwards, you should probably follow up with diamonds or something." She started laughing as I stood to leave.

"Or a baby."

"Come again." My mom pretended to clean her ears out.

"I can give her a baby."

"Boy, I know damn well you didn't get her pregnant on purpose."

"Yes the fuck I did and if she's not, I'm gonna keep doing it until she is."

"Let me find out you tryna trap her."

"Call it what you want but what she got in between her legs; another man won't ever know." She threw a dishrag at me and told me to get out.

I don't care what no one says, that's my woman and I'll be damned if I lose her for some fuck shit I did. Now, all I have to do is figure out a way to win her back.

Luna

"Somebody better tell me what the fuck is going on before there's three dead bodies on the ground." Waleed had his gun pointed on me but little did he know, there were about ten on him. See, Oscar never traveled alone and neither did I. I'm sure my father's people are here as well.

"Waleed, put the gun down and let me explain."

"Nah." He cocked it back and now placed it on my temple. I had to hurry and diffuse the situation because I'm not sure what my father had planned.

"Fuck her Waleed! This bitch is married and you're with me. Why does it matter?" His hand went back and Julie was on the ground. He literally knocked her the fuck out, but why? All she did was speak the truth.

It didn't take long for gunfire to erupt. Waleed, grabbed my hand and had me hide behind a car. He returned fire and all hell broke loose. Suburban's were pulling up and men were jumping out. He looked at me and I shrugged my shoulders. I never actually told him what my father was into or why bodyguards followed wherever I went. We weren't close enough but if he were to ask me now, I'd tell him. But then again, maybe not.

"Get in." He opened a door to a building and had me go inside. I heard it lock and turned around.

"Oh shit. You're hit." Blood was dripping down his arm.

"I'm fine." Just like a man to downplay things. I took his shirt off and saw blood leaking profusely from two spots.

"Fuck! Let me call my father."

"For what? I'm fine." His words started slurring

"No you're not." I heard the phone ringing and once my father picked up, he started asking if I were ok and where was I.

"Daddy, trace my phone. I'm in a building and Waleed's been hit; twice. He needs a doctor."

"Ok. I'll send someone for you." I hung up and used my hand to put pressure on it.

"Why did you save me?" He was going in and out and here I was asking questions.

"Because no one's gonna kill you but me." His hand were on the side of my face.

"Are you serious right now?"

"Yup. I'm gonna watch you die slow too." He used his other hand and pulled my face to his.

"You better be the first fucking person I see, when I wake up." He kissed me and you could hear the door being kicked open. Men came running in and raced out the door with Waleed. My dad checked me over to make sure I wasn't shot.

"Where are they taking him?" I pointed to the guys pulling off in the black truck, with Waleed inside.

"He'll be fine Luna. I need to get you home. Your mother is worried."

"I'll call her. Please take me to him."

"Luna."

"Please." He looked at me and called one of the guys over.

"Take her to the spot and I'll meet you there shortly."
He yoked the guy up.

"If anything, and I mean anything happens to my daughter, I'm gonna cut your head off, put it on a spike and set it in front of your house for your family to see. Am I clear?" The guy was petrified.

"I think he gets it." I pulled my dad's hands off his shirt and followed him out the door. There were cops down the street, along with ambulances and a bunch of detectives.

It took a while to get to the place he had Waleed. It made me worry because if it took us this long, how could he make it with all the blood loss? Then I thought about how he still made threats of killing me. That man is a trip but I'm in love with him.

The driver opened the door and helped me step out. Shockingly, my mom was standing by the door.

She ran over and checked me over to make sure I wasn't hit too. Afterwards, we stepped inside and, in a room, where I could see the doctors operating on Waleed. I thought about contacting Risky but I'm not sure my dad would be ok with him coming here. And I know he wouldn't stay away. Then I still needed to call Khloe back as well. She called and sent a message saying something happened to her mother but with everything going on it totally slipped my mind.

"He's gonna be fine Luna." My mom wiped my eyes and rubbed my shoulders. I knew he would be because his evil ass couldn't die. At least, not until he found out the truth, which is why he probably wanted me there when he woke up.

"Are you hungry?"

"No." I stared at the doctors and smiled as they pulled the bullets out.

"What happened out there?" I began to tell her when my father walked in. He appeared to be angrier than I've ever seen.

"Luna, did you know your so-called man was sleeping with Julie?" My mom gasped and covered his mouth.

"I found out a couple of weeks ago when I walked in on them."

"Mija, I'm sorry." My mom hugged me.

"She still trying to hurt me but how did Julie find out about Waleed? We don't hang in the same circle." My father lifted my face.

"She's obviously been watching you. And if she bed him, the two of them had to have known one another prior to you." I nodded because that had to be the reason.

"Did he ever mention her? Does he have any photos lying around of them? How much do you really know about him?" I knew he was questioning me because believe it or not, I've never had a boyfriend.

Growing up my father was super, over protective and never allowed me to do anything without being watched. I understood and never complained. However, as I got older, my ass became curious about guys. Instead of going to him, I went to my mother and she told me enough. She also gave me the birds and the bees speech and said, eventually; I'll be ready for sex but needed to be protected. My mom brought me condoms and even put me on birth control behind my father's back. She too thought he was overboard. Unfortunately, being the head of one of the most ruthless and deadliest cartel in the world, we had no choice but to abide by his rules.

Well one day, Khloe and I were at her house and her parents were away for the night. They never went on vacation because Khloe was young and being a daddy's girl, her father never wanted to be far. Anyway, she and I may have been chunky growing up but we were cool as hell with all the guys at school. We invited two of the closest ones over and started playing truth or dare. The bottle landed on me and let's just say me and dude definitely went through with the dare. He broke my virginity and the two of us had sex plenty of times after that. No one knew and we wanted to keep it that way. Sadly, he was sent to jail for murder and up until I got with Waleed, we stayed in touch.

I wrote him a letter and let him know we had to stop communicating as much. He'd call once or twice a week and we'd talk for as long as the guard would let him stay on his phone. He understood because even though he was in jail for the last ten years, he got married and had two kids. The woman and I were cool and I even watched the kids on a few occasions for her to go see him. People may say it's crazy but he and I were more best friends than anything. She respected our friendship and I did the same for their relationship. Plus, he really was in love with her and shockingly, the feelings were mutual. Of course, I kept eyes on her for him. What kind of friend would I be if I didn't?

"I know enough about him daddy."

"And what's that?"

"I know where he lives, the passcode to his phone, house and his safes. I'm aware of him receiving product and on what days. I also know about the ex-bitter bitch Dora. I've met his mother and some of his other family members and I do know how much money he has in his bank account and the two he has overseas. I also know, he never slept with anyone else because he was with me damn near every day, all day. I'm just not sure how I missed this shit with Julie." I looked back down and the doctor was sewing him up.

"Maybe you didn't miss it."

"What you mean mommy?"

"I'm saying. Maybe she's always been there but he never mentioned her. I doubt he knew she was your sister but she for sure knew about the two of you." My mom said rubbing my back. She obviously wanted me to be with Waleed because she surely had his back.

"Why wouldn't he tell me?"

"Honey, people hold things in if they feel they're not worthy of speaking on. You only know about the Dora chick because she hangs with the heffa his friend is dealing with." My father handed me an envelope.

"What's this?"

"Give this to Waleed when he's better. He'll know what to do with it." I opened it and saw photos of Veronica and some big black dude. There were a few of Dora as well, with the same guy. The last photo was of Veronica coming out of a doctor's office. I looked in the envelope and emptied out the rest of the contents. There was a medical record with my sisters' name on it. I was about to look when the doctor the stepped in. He mentioned Waleed would be fine and if I wanted to take him home, I could. The question is, did I want to?

"Daddy."

"They're placing him in the ambulance. He'll be at your house and set up when you get there." I hugged him and grabbed the stuff he handed me. I know its not safe to move him after surgery but he wouldn't wanna be here when he woke up. I know for a fact he would want Risky here as well, to discuss it. There's no doubt in my mind that he'll be ready for war.

"Luna, I still want you leaving with us." He was very adamant when he made that statement.

"How can I?"

"Honey, Oscar is in town and I'm not sure it's for a good cause." He stared at me with both hands on my shoulder.

"Let me make sure he's fine and we can discuss it. I won't leave him like this." He nodded and moved out the way.

"Are you pregnant?" I froze when my mom asked. I heard her shoes walking behind me. I knew it was her because my dad had on sneakers.

"Whyyyyy... why... did you ask me that?" My back was still turned away from them.

"Because your belly is a little bigger, you cried over your dad asking questions about coming with us and you've been eating these nasty ass vegetables on the table, even after you told me you weren't hungry." I shook my head laughing. I don't even know where the urge to eat came from but I was starving.

"Yes." I turned around and both of my parents were smiling.

"Oh my God. I'm gonna be a Gma. I'm so excited. How far along are you? Do you know if is a girl or boy? What are the names you have picked out? Does Waleed know?" The questions were non-stop from her. My father came closer and put both hands on my face.

"I'm not happy because you were promised to another man but I understand."

"I don't know what to do? Oscar isn't going to let me keep this baby and Waleed won't allow me to terminate it. He wants kids and..." He shushed me with his index finger.

"You are not to tell anyone right now. Do you understand?" I nodded.

"As far as Oscar, I have plans for him and your sister."

"Can I tell Waleed and Khloe?"

"No one else. I don't want anyone trying to make you lose my grandchild." He kissed my forehead and told me to go take care of Waleed and they'd be by tomorrow.

I jumped in the truck, laid my head backed and thought of ways to inform him about the pregnancy. The last time I tried to talk to him, he went out and fucked my ho ass sister. Which reminds me. He is gonna tell me what their affiliation is, whether he wants to or not.

Waleed

"How is he?" I heard my mom ask someone.

"He's good. The doctor said once the anesthesia wears off, he'll be up. The bullets both went in and exited out his back."

"Are you ok? Did you tell him?" I opened my eyes and noticed them smiling.

"Tell me what?" I tried to sit up and they both came over.

"Hey baby." My mom said and kissed my cheek. Luna had her arms folded and stood off to the side. I know her ass ain't made after the shit I heard. My ass may have been shot but I didn't forget the conversation beforehand.

"I'm good. Ma, can you give us some time to talk. We both have things to say." I kept my eyes on Luna.

My mom closed the door and I insisted on getting up to use the bathroom. While I was in there, I couldn't help but think about the shit that went down. How is she married and fucking me on the regular? We're always together in and out the house and no one has ever approached her about another woman or her regarding another man. The most mind-boggling shit outta all this is, her and Julie being sisters. How in the hell is that even possible? Luna, never mentioned a sister and Julie damn sure didn't. Did they hate each other that much?

After using the bathroom, I reached in the shower area to turn it on and heard the door open. Luna walked over, helped me out my clothes and removed the shower head so my arm wouldn't get wet. I allowed her to wash me up and watched as she took her time. Mad and all, she was still taking care of me and a nigga truly appreciated it.

Once the soap was rinsed off, she dried my body and wrapped a towel around my waist. When I stepped in the room, there were a pair of sweats, a wife beater, boxers and socks on the bed. She made her way over to me and assisted in what I needed. Sad to say, my dick got hard each time she stepped away.

"You good." She picked my bloody clothes up and tossed them in a trash bag. She said, my mom changed the sheets and was downstairs cooking me some food.

"Sit down Luna." I patted the seat next to me on the bed. She refused at first, but once I gave her the look, she did.

"Why did you run to another woman?" And just like that, the questions I knew she'd want answers to, started.

"Luna, it wasn't supposed to happen."

"But it did."

"You're right but let me explain." She rolled her eyes.

"I went to the liquor store, brought some Henney and went straight home. Julie must've been waiting because once I got to my door, she came behind me. I told her to bounce, shut the door in her face and walked upstairs to shower. I planned on getting pissy drunk and calling you." She chuckled.

"I was. Unfortunately, I didn't lock the door, she snuck in the shower and sucked me off. I was mad at you and didn't even try to fight. I told her to leave and as you saw, things escalated."

"So you're telling me that you sleep around when you're mad?"

"Look at me." I lifted her face.

"Julie and I were a couple some years ago. She did something, I'm not willing to forgive and I cut her off. I hadn't spoken to her in years and all of a sudden she showed up for whatever reason."

"A couple? Waleed, why didn't you tell me?"

"Like you mentioned being married?"

"It's not what you think and contrary to what you think, I didn't hop in bed with anyone. I came rushing over here to explain why I called you but it was too late. I was so hurt because not only did you hang up on me but were you enjoying it."

"Do you know the bitch knew I was at the door and smirked as she was riding you?

"Luna." It tore me up to see how upset she saw me giving another woman the business, especially; her sister.

"I know we weren't a couple and you don't owe me an explanation but I know she did it to get back at me."

"What?" She explained how they had different moms and lived together at one point but Julie tried to kill her mom. She was kicked out the house with nothing and they never saw her again. Somewhere in that time, I must've met her but never did she mention any family. I knew her mother passed and her father was supposedly a deadbeat but that's as much as she told me and I never bothered to look into it.

"Do you love her?"

"Do you love him?"

"You can't ask a question with a question." I laughed because I always hit her with that line.

"I used to love her. A lotta time passed and my any love I had for her, faded away."

"Then why sleep with her?"

"Nah. It's your turn. Do you love him?"

"No and I never did."

"Why did you sleep with her?" She went right back to the question.

"I was being stupid and a man. I didn't even know you were there and I'm sorry for hurting you." I used my thumb to wipe the tear that fell.

"I never should've let it get that far and whether I asked you to be my girl or not, in my eyes you were."

"So you cheated?"

"No because after the phone call I assumed you cheated on me and said, fuck it.

"Whatever." She waved me off.

"Tell me about this Oscar dude." I was flabbergasted with the story. Her pops was on some old fashioned type shit and now she's caught up in the middle of a war. I say a war because there's no way I'm letting what went down slide.

"Why did Julie say you were married?" I needed to know because I ain't being a side nigga for no chick.

"I'm supposed to marry him in two months."

"Well that ain't happening." She smirked.

"And why not?"

"Don't play with me Luna." I grabbed her hand with my good one and had her stand in front of me.

65

"All this is mine and contract or not, he'll never get it again." I used both of my hands the best I could and unbuttoned her jeans. Surprisingly, there were marks on her stomach from being too tight. I've never seen these on her. Luna made sure her clothes were fit correctly so I'm a little shocked.

"Waleed." I rubbed the marks and felt something wet hit my face. She had tears coming down her face as if something were wrong.

"Why are your jeans so tight?"

"I haven't had time to shop for new clothes yet." I looked up at her wiping her face.

"New clothes for what?" She shrugged her shoulders.

"I'm pregnant."

"Say word."

"Word." She handed me the paperwork from the doctors. I read the part where it said positive and she was approximately twelve weeks, which means she's been pregnant for a minute and neither of us knew. I kissed her belly and stood.

"Don't let me catch you in no more tight clothes. How the hell my baby supposed to breathe?"

"You're not upset?"

"Hell no. Yo, I told Risky you'd be pregnant first."

"WHAT?"

"Yup. He's tryna get Khloe pregnant." She started laughing.

"Damn. I'm about to be a father. You keeping it right?"

"Ugh Yea. My parents and your mom won't even let me think about aborting it."

"What you doing?" I used my good hand to unsnap her bra.

"We need to celebrate and this is a perfect way to start."

"Oh yea." She walked over and locked the door. All her clothes were off before making it back to me and my dick stood at attention.

"Did you use condoms with her? I can't risk our baby's health..." She stood over me after pulling my boxers and sweats down.

"Hell yea. This the only pussy I'm running in raw." I guided her down and enjoyed the way she rode me.

"Let me eat that." She was about to get on the bed when someone knocked on the door.

"Dammit." Luna hopped off, grabbed her clothes and ran in the bathroom. I pulled my clothes up, checked to make sure none of her stuff was on the floor and opened the door.

"When we rolling out?" Risky walked in with Khloe behind.

"Where's Luna?" She had an attitude and her arms were folded across her chest. You would think I did something to her by the way she was acting.

"Damn. Can I get a hello or, how are you?"

"Yea, Yea. Where she at?" She moved closer to the bathroom.

"Yo, you rude as hell."

"Says the nigga who knocked on the door when me and him were fucking a while back."

"Oh that was different."

"How?" She folded her arms.

68

"Because you were on some ho shit."

"What the fuck you say?" She came closer to me.

"You didn't even know him and was in the bathroom giving it up."

"And you're a minute man." Risky busted out laughing.

"Ask yo girl if I'm a minute man."

"Whatever. Move." She pushed me.

"Owwwwwwwww."

"Oh shit. My bad." She had a sad look on her face, thinking she hurt me.

"I was just playing."

"Ughhhhhh."

"Why you keep messing with my girl like that?" Risky was shaking his head laughing. I wasn't disrespecting her and the two of us stayed going at it. It was all love tho.

"Oh she your girl?"

"She's my girl but I ain't her man." We both laughed.

"I have to come up with something to win her over. I fucked up."

"Hell fucking yea, you did. Then you had th nerve to get my girl involved. Oh shit, Luna pregnant."

"Really?"

"Yup, she just told me." He reached in his pocket and peeled off five hundred dollars. The bet was whoever got their chick pregnant first had to pay up. I didn't need it but we weren't the type of dudes who didn't pay a debt.

"I think Khloe was taking those pills because I nut in her the first time we had sex, and never stopped." I looked to the bathroom door and they were coming out.

"Hell yea, she did." I couldn't elaborate more without the Luna and Khloe asking questions but he's right. If Khloe isn't pregnant, she definitely did something to stop it or had an abortion, which I know for a fact he'd be pissed if she did. I know a plan b can stop a pregnancy but an abortion is different.

"Congratulations, punk." Khloe pushed on my good shoulder.

"Thanks, and I'm sure he'll knock you up soon."

"He ain't knocking up shit because his dick won't be in me ever again." She mushed me in the head and walked downstairs with Luna.

"You're gonna have to do a hell of a lot to even get her alone in a room." I started cracking up, while he was sitting there tryna figure out what he could do to fix it.

"Anyway, lets discuss this shit. Who the fuck is Oscar and when you ready to get at him?"

"Soon as I heal, we can go in but we'll have t be careful."

"What you mean?" I walked over, closed the door ad filled him in on the information Luna gave me. There is about to be a big ass war soon and we had to be ready or someone will be burying us, in his funeral home instead of the other way around.

Lamar

"I don't care what you say ma. He's the reason Lacey's dead and Raina tried to kill herself." My mom had stopped by my house to discuss the shit between Risky and I. Everyone in the streets knew what went on between us and someone told her. When she asked me, I wasn't gonna tell her but since she asked it was up to me to tell her.

After he pulled a gun on me at the hospital, it only fueled the fire in me. Veronica came up with a plan to hit him where it hurts and at first, I was skeptical. Not because of being scared but the person she was tryna drag in, isn't a threat. However, once shit popped off at the hospital, it was a wrap. I'm gonna make sure he suffers and allow my niece to stay with me and my mom full time.

"Lamar what happened to your sister was very unfortunate and there's not a day that goes by where she's not on my mind. But ask yourself, if whatever scheme your coming up with will benefit you. Am I gonna be allowed to see

72

my grandchild? Are you going to die in the process? Or will it bring my daughter back?" She stood there with her arms folded.

"Ma, he violated on all levels by pulling a gun out on me."

"Really? From what you say he had every right to."

"Are you serious?" I was pissed and pacing back and forth in the kitchen.

"Lamar, you can't blame him for things he wasn't around for." I thought about what she said and couldn't help but reminisce on the death of my sister.

"Have you seen Ryan?" Lacey was crying in the phone.

"No. Why what's up?"

"I got a bad feeling Lamar."

"What you mean?" I loved my sister to death and being we were twins, I'd do anything for her. But she had a bad feeling anytime her nigga left the house.

"I know, I say it all the time but this time it's different." I heard panic in her voice.

"Where's Raina?" My niece was five at the time. Her and Ryan were together for some years and I can honestly say,

he's never cheated on her to my knowledge. Being around

them used to make all of us sick because they were always

lovey dovey. He even proposed to her. Sadly, the wedding

never happened.

"She with his mom. I'm going to find him."

"Lacey no." I had already started putting my clothes

on because I knew she'd try to send me out. But when she

offered herself, I had to intervene. See, I worked for Risky and

knew tonight was the night he retired. He hadn't told her yet

because it was a surprise. He was done with the street life,

wanted to marry her, have more kids and live on some happily

ever after shit.

"I'll go."

"I'm already in the car. I traced his phone to some

warehouse."

"Lacey just stay home. I'll go and have him call you."

"I just need to see he's ok." I heard the car start and

hurried to mine.

"Lacey wait." She hung up and I tried to reach Risky
but he didn't answer. I knew he wouldn't because the guy he
met with never allowed phones in their meetings.

I rushed over to the warehouse and saw Lacey getting
out her car. I also saw men dressed in black coming in her
direction with guns drawn and telling her to stop. Lacey was
screaming that she wanted to see Ryan but none of them
listened. Sadly she continued walking and bullets flew,
catching her in the upper torso. I ran over and held my hands
up so they wouldn't shoot.

"Fuck. Go get Risky."

"Who the fuck are you and this bitch?" Some guy said
and when I looked, I had no idea who he was, which meant he
was from the other guys team.

"Lacey please don't die."

*"You better fucking answer or you'll be dead with
her."* I felt a gun on the back of my skull.

*"This is Risky's fiancé and I'm her brother. She needs
an ambulance."* I had my hand on her chest but blood was

gushing out from her stomach and legs. I heard a guy speaking

another language on the walker talkie.

"I should've listened to you Lamar." She whispered.

"It's ok Lacey. You're gonna be fine."

"Please watch over Raina with him. Protect her with

everything you have."

"Stop talking like that." Her eyes began to flutter.

"WHAT THE FUCK HAPPENED?" I heard Risky yell.

He dropped to his knees and the tears started falling.

"Oh shit." Waleed helped Risky lift her up and ran to

one of the trucks. They put her in and sped out.

I met them at the hospital along with my mom, his and

Raina. There were guards blocking the entrance and it took a

minute for him to come get us. The look on his face towards me

was of pure hate. I knew he would blame me but I had nothing

to do with it.

A few hours later, the doctor informed us of what we

already knew. Lacey died from multiple gunshot wounds. Risky

charged me and had my ass against the wall with a gun under

my chin. I told him over and over I didn't send her but he

refused to listen. After everyone got him off me; my mom and I
stayed at the hospital to identify her body. Of course Risky
picked the body up from there and had the service in his
funeral home.

It took a long time for us to speak again and we only
did on the strength of Raina. Waleed had me working under
him but the money wasn't shit. I wanted more and that's why
Dora and I went to that trap house to rob his ass. There was no
beef with Waleed or Wale as we call him but I wanted it all.
And being Risky was going to marry my sister, he should've
handed it over to me.

If you wanna know why I blame him, it's because had
he answered his fucking phone, Lacey would've never gone
searching for him. Therefore; he is responsible for her death
and I've been tryna find ways to avenge it. Now that he's with
someone else, it's only fair to take someone he loves away
from him.

"Ma, if he answered the phone she'd be alive." She
walked over to me.

"He told her his phone would be off. Son, you have to let it go."

"How do you know?"

"She told me."

"What?" Now I was really confused.

"I asked her not to go too Lamar but she didn't listen. You know your sister always acted off impulse."

"Are you blaming Lacey?"

"Not at all but she knew the risks being with a man like him. She also knew not to ever go around his work."

"Come on ma." She put her hands on my face.

"I loved my daughter with all my heart but if she stayed her ass home, she may be here. And who's to say she wouldn't have done it another time?"

"I can't believe you're talking like this." She shook her head.

"God don't make mistakes Lamar and I'm telling you to let it go before I have two deceased children." She turned and walked away, leaving me standing there stuck on stupid. Should I leave well enough alone?

****

"Good morning." I approached the chick. She was definitely fat like Veronica said but she was beautiful and carried herself well.

The night Veronica and I slept together, she asked me to help her with something and she'd reward me with sex. Like any man, who gives up a free offer of sex. Especially, when the sex is good. Yea, she may be friends with my girl Dora, but I also know she gets high and if I caught her at the right time, I'd get ti fuck and sure enough, its exactly how it went down. I give it to Veronica though. She knew how to lay it down on a nigga but in my opinion, Dora still had the best shit, which is why I wasn't satisfied after sleeping with her and slept with my girl.

Anyway, she asked me to try and befriend some chick named Khloe who was stepping on her toes with Risky as she put it. When I asked what she meant, she only said, the bitch needed to die or get in a bad car accident where no one would recognize her. Killing her isn't something I wanted to do because she did absolutely nothing to me but causing a car accident is nothing. I've done that a few times to some of the butches I fucked that never called me back. They had the nerve to say what we shared was a one-night stand. Yea, well that's not my motto and they definitely learned after the situations I caused.

One chick, I cut her brake lines because she called me an ugly, black gorilla looking nigga and she'd never give me the time of day. Guess it don't matter now because her ass is in a wheelchair. The second chick, is the one who told me we were a one-night stand. Well, she was one night for sure because I snuck in her crib one night, set it on fire and left the gasoline can on the living room floor. The fire inspector claimed it to be arson and her ass is in jail. Another chick had the audacity to tell me I couldn't eat pussy well. Shit, I put a gun to her head and made her lick my ass until I came. Hell yea, I liked that shit and so did every other man. They won't say it but secretly every man wants it done. Long story short, any woman who treated me like shit regretted it and I loved every minute of watching them suffer. Oh what y'all thought only women get in their feelings? Nah, when a bitch tries and play a man, he gets upset too.

"Good morning. Thanks for holding the door.

"Anytime for your sexy ass." She sucked her teeth.

"Why you doing all that?" I followed behind her to some Mercedes truck.

"You could've just said you're welcome and kept it moving. Why be disrespectful?"

"Disrespectful? That's nowhere near disrespectful."

"So you licking your lips and eyeing my titties isn't disrespectful or you being in my personal space blowing your nasty ass breath in my face, ain't either. Righttttt." I put my hand to my face, blew my breath and almost passed out my damn self. It did stink but she didn't have to say it.

"It smells like you been eating ass or something." She opened the door and I noticed how nice her ass sat in those jeans.

"Bitch, I suggest…"

"Bitch?" She questioned with her hand on her hips.

"That's what I said."

"Oh yea." She reached in her truck and I attempted to reach for my gun but it was too late. This trick sprayed the fuck outta me with mace and ended up leaving. I made sure to get her license plate number because a nigga is damn sure gonna see her again. I wiped my eyes and went to my car. I heard a knock on my window and looked up to see some Mexican looking nigga at me. I rolled my window down. *What the fuck did he want?*

Khloe

"Hey Marcus. How are you?" I gave him a hug and he searched behind me.

"He's not here." I could see the relief as he sat down. I called to apologize about the way Ryan treated him at the club and at first, he wanted nothing to do with me. Once I told him we weren't together, he agreed to meet.

"Khloe, I have to ask."

"What?" I glanced over the menu the waitress handed us and waited for the question.

"Why are you with a guy like him? You're smart, beautiful and independent. You can do so much better." I sat the menu down.

"If I'm all that, why did you cheat?"

"Khloe!"

"And have babies on me. Was I not good enough? Why couldn't you wait?" I felt myself becoming upset because even though I forgave him, it still hurt.

83

"I was young Khloe and you were a virgin."

"And?"

"And I messed up."

"Messing up is one thing but two you had two babies?"
I took a sip of the water.

"Khloe, I never meant to hurt you and I'm truly, truly
sorry. I know you forgave me but did you really?"

"To be honest, I did. However, it still hurts when I
think about it."

"But we weren't even discussing it."

"Once you mentioned me deserving better, it brought
back memories and made me ask why you didn't treat me
better." He put his hands on top of mine.

"How could I mess up with you?" He leaned over the
table and planted a kiss on my lips. Instead of pushing him
away, I grabbed his face and allowed our tongues to have fun.
We heard someone clear their throat and turned to see the
waitress grinning.

"Can we get this to go?" I asked and started picking my
things up. Was I worried about Ryan? *Hell fucking no.* He ain't

my man and I'm not about to be with him because he said sorry and loved me.

The night Raina went in the hospital, he was very upset and I stayed by his side. Not because I wanted to be with him but because he needed all the support he could get. Then he stayed at my house and there was barely any interaction. Now his daughter has gone through some other things and I was there for him again. He said, he loved me and he may but in this case; actions speak louder than words and so far, nothing.

I may be a bigger woman but my feelings matter. Just because he's in a different head space it doesn't mean, I'm gonna welcome him with open arms and forget the disrespect. Shit, he told his ex he don't fuck fat bitches. I swear it broke my heart in a million pieces to hear him say that. All the times we spent together obviously meant nothing to him. They couldn't have if he said that.

Now I blame myself too because I knew he was ashamed of me and still allowed him to bed me. I guess sleeping with someone so sexy, fascinated me and my morals and self-respect went out the window. I worked too hard to be a strong plus size woman and even though it was for a short time, I'm not losing my self-worth any longer. If he can't accept my body and not just behind closed doors, then he can keep it pushing.

****

I pulled up at the hotel with Marcus behind me. I didn't think he'd come but here we are taking the key from the receptionist and headed towards the elevator. Once we stepped off and entered the room, we were all over each other. I was definitely horny and I guess he was too.

"Are you sure Khloe?" He asked placing kisses on my neck.

"Yes, now fuck me." He lifted his head and smirked. His pants and boxers hit the floor and so did my clothes.

"Just as I remember." He licked his lips and led me to the bed. I opened my legs and watched him go to work on my pussy. I don't ever recall him giving me head this well and I'm not complaining.

"You missed me." He wiped his face and grabbed a condom. Hell yea we stopped by a store on the way. I was careless as hell sleeping with Ryan unprotected but it won't happen with Marcus.

"No." I grabbed his arms and felt him push his way in.

"No?" He sounded a little upset with my answer but it was true. I did miss him after finding out but as time went on, I didn't miss a thing.

"I didn't Marcus."

"I missed you."

"Ok can you just fuck me?" He nodded and once we found our rhythm, we literally wore each other out. We took a shower together and ordered takeout. Room service wasn't going to be there for an hour tho.

As were sitting there watching a movie and waiting on the food, my phone rang and it was Raina. What is she doing up this late?

"Hey Raina." Marcus was rubbing my feet.

"Are you picking me up tomorrow? I asked daddy and he said, you're not talking to him. Was he mean to you?"

"No Raina, he wasn't. Your dad and I are only friends and we didn't talk because we've both been busy."

"Ok because I told him, I'm still living with you." I started laughing.

"Why are you up anyway? It's after midnight."

"I had a nightmare." I hated that she was having them and we still haven't found Veronica.

"Did you tell your dad?"

"Yea he's right here." I smiled knowing he wasn't out with some tramp.

"Well you know he's not going to let anything happen to you."

"I know. Hold on." I heard some noises in the background.

"I'll be right back Raina." Ryan said and his voice made me hot all over again.

"Khloe."

"Yesssss." I moaned out a little when Marcus started playing with my pussy.

"I wanna ask you something."

"Ok." I tried to hold my moans in but Marcus was making it very hard.

"Was it worth it?"

"I don't know what you mean. Was what worth it?"

"Was that fuck worth him losing his life?" I sat up and pushed Marcus off me. I stood and began looking around the room for cameras or anything to indicate he was there or watching me.

"Ryan."

"Ryan?" Marcus whispered and hopped off the bed. He grabbed his clothes.

"Oh that nigga remembers me?"

"Ryan what are you talking about?" I tried to play dumb but it wasn't working because Ryan could hear the nervousness through the phone.

"You think I don't know you're at the Hilton fucking that nigga? Huh?"

"Are you watching me?" He laughed.

"Nah K. I'm home with my daughter but someone else is watching you." I turned around and Marcus was opening the door.

"DONT OPEN THE DOOR!" I shouted. Unfortunately, it was too late. Two men came in and were now beating the crap out of him. Marcus had no chance.

"Ryan tell them to stop."

"Why would I do that?" He was hysterical laughing in the phone as if he could see everything going down.

"Ryan please."

"You love him K?" I looked at my phone. Why was he asking me some stupid shit instead of calling his goons off?

"Ryan stop this."

"DO YOU LOVE HIM KHLOE? WAS IT WORTH IT?" I saw Waleed walked in and place a gun on Marcus forehead.

"NO! I DONT LOVE HIM. PLEASE MAKE THEM STOP." I was hysterical crying.

"If you ever cheat on me again, I'm gonna kill you and him. Do I make myself clear?" *Cheating. We're not even a couple.*

"Ok Ryan. Please stop this."

"Give Waleed the phone." I did like he asked and pushed the guys back.

"Nah, she tryna nurse him back to health."

PHEW!

"AHHHHH." Marcus yelled out and I looked to see he had a bullet in his kneecap.

"Nah, she still down there."

PHEW! Marcus screamed out again.

"WALEED STOP."

"This last one is gonna kill him K. You need to move."

"OK. OK. I GET IT RYAN. I FUCKING GET IT." I moved away from Marcus and Waleed pulled the gun back. He handed me the phone and a blanket. All I had on was a long T-shirt. You couldn't see anything but still.

"Get the fuck up, take your ass with Waleed and I'll see you when you get here."

"I'm not.-" The phone hung up. I tossed it across the room and sat there.

"Look Khloe. I'm not in the mood and my girl, your best friend is getting on my nerves tryna find out if you're ok. I suggest you get it together and let me drop you off."

"And what if I don't wanna go?" He had an evil smirk on his face.

"Let's just say, if he has to come get you it won't be pretty." I looked up at him and refused to take any chances on Ryan showing up. I stood, took my clothes in the bathroom and got dressed.

"I'm ready." All three of them stared at me.

"Oh shit yo. He's gonna be pisssssssed." One of the guys said and covered his mouth with his hand.

"Khloe, I'm gonna have Luna pray for you."

"What? Why?"

"This dumb nigga left three big ass hickeys on your neck." I ran back in the bathroom to look and sure enough my neck was covered.

"Waleed, can't you talk to him?"

"HELL NO. THAT NIGGA CRAZY!" They thought it was funny.

"Is he really gonna kill me?"

"Khloe, you fucked up is all I'm gonna say but I will tell Luna you loved her and died happy." I sucked my teeth and pushed past him.

"Hey don't get tough with me lady. You better save that energy for when Ryan sees you." Waleed said in a voice that could portray my father. I stepped out the room and saw a few big guys dressed in black coming in our direction. They spoke and went into my room.

"Take me home." Waleed pressed the elevator button and stared at me.

"What?" I was staring at the lights on the elevator light up as we passed each floor.

"I know he was foul as hell for hiding you and you have every right to move on." He stopped.

"But?" I looked over at him.

"But he loves you. Matter of fact, he's in love with you and when he loves, he loves hard." I stood there listening to him.

"I'm in love with him too but he messed up and what he did tonight won't make me want him." I stepped off the elevator and followed Waleed to his truck. I got inside and we drove in silence. Once he pulled up in front of Ryan's mother house, my heart began to beat fast.

"Can you come in with me?"

"Ummm no. I don't wanna witness no domestic violence tonight. Peace." He put up his two fingers and told me to get out. The front door opened and Ryan leaned on the frame. I really hope he didn't kill me.

Risky

Looking at Khloe get out the truck with Waleed only pissed me off more. Those hickeys were big as day and all I wanted to do is wring her fucking neck. I shouldn't be mad because we aren't together in her eyes but it doesn't mean go sleep with someone else either. I had plans for us and here she standing here with sex all over her. The funny part is she's scared as hell and she should be.

"Ryan..." I put my hand up.

"Take my truck and get the fuck out my face." I knew her car was at the hotel and she'd need a ride home but I was taking her.

"Who the hell?" I towered over her.

"You think I'm playing with you?" I put the keys in her hand and turned her around. She tried going in to see Raina but my daughter ain't stupid and those marks will cause her to ask questions. I started walking to Waleed who was sitting there laughing with his doofy ass, like always.

"Ryan, you act like..."

"I act like what? Huh?" I ran up on her.

"I act like a nigga who gives a fuck about you. A nigga who knows all about your past with that punk. You talk about me disrespecting you and he had a whole family on you."

"That's in the past."

"Oh, so you're that forgiving?"

"It's been years."

"So the fuck what."

"So it means I can do what I want. Ryan were not together and the shit you did tonight won't make me want you." I chuckled.

"Let me make something clear for you." I pushed her towards my truck because looking at her neck was pissing me off even more.

"You got some good pussy and even made me fall in love with yo ass but don't get it twisted. I can fuck any bitch out here and won't have to worry about them sleeping with the next nigga to piss me off.

"I didn't.-"

96

"Yes the fuck you did but the joke is on you because I knew. I know all about the phone calls and him not even wanting to meet at first. The dinner at the restaurant and you fucking him."

"Why do you even care? Fat bitches aren't in your future, right? You wanna continue fucking me and possibly get me pregnant to keep my legs closed but guess what?" She closed the door to the truck.

"You and I won't be together because you're ashamed of me. And..." I just walked away from her.

In the beginning, I was ashamed but after falling in love, there was no way I could deny her. She loved my daughter and being with a bigger woman doesn't ruin my reputation. I guess those video vixen bitches had my mind clouded. Veronica didn't help either by reminding me every chance she got on Khloe's size.

"RYAN! RYAN!" She shouted. I sat in the truck with Waleed and took a few pulls from the blunt. I laid my head on the seat and closed my eyes.

"RISKY!" She yelled my street name and opened the door.

"What Khloe?"

"I wasn't finished talking."

"But I was finished listening so take yo ass home."

"Yea." Waleed chiming in only angered her.

"Shut up Waleed and I'm gonna tell Luna how you were all in our business." She had her hands on her hips. She knew Luna would get in his ass about being in the middle.

"How the hell you telling her that and not me shooting out your ex kneecaps."

"Ughhhh, y'all both make me sick." I blew smoke in the air.

"Go home Khloe." I said and she refused to move from the spot.

"When I'm done talking."

"Fine! Say what you need to before I choke the shit outta you."

"You're not choking shit." I handed Waleed the blunt back and got out the car. She backed up once she noticed my face.

"Why did you send those people there to hurt Marcus?" I walked over to my truck and opened the door.

"RYAN!"

"WHAT KHLOE? WHAT THE FUCK YOU WANT ME TO SAY?"

"Say what you mean."

"You wanna know what I mean." I folded my arms.

"I told you I loved you Khloe. I'm not saying it meant you forgave me and I get it. Trust me, I do. I probably fucked your head up and I am truly regretful for it. But instead of either waiting for me or even finding someone new, you hop in the bed with the same nigga who hurt you worse than me."

"Ryan?"

"Nah you wanted to know so let me finish." She nodded.

"Then you were by my side with Raina and a nigga appreciates that more than you know. I apologized and told you I'm gonna spend every day tryna make you forgive me."

"But you didn't."

"Khloe you didn't give me time. I had to make sure Raina was good before going all out for you." She couldn't say shit because her and everyone else knew, I was back and forth with therapy and trying my hardest to get Raina to open up about who was touching her.

"I mean damn it's only been a few weeks and you fucked someone else. And before you talk shit, I've had dry dick since you caught me and Ronny."

"I find that hard to believe."

"I don't give a fuck what you believe but what I do care about is, if you didn't want this then you should've told me at the hospital when I apologized. K, I'll say it a million times. I know I hurt you real bad and that's something I'm dealing with but like I said, I can't rock with a chick who seeks out another man to piss me off." She tried to speak.

"Say what you want, but we both know the truth."

There was nothing she could say because it's the truth.

"Now can you leave? I'll pick my truck up tomorrow." I stepped away and heard her yelling out for me again. I noticed Waleed get out his truck and head towards her. I sat down and picked the blunt up. I could hear them talking.

"Khloe, not right now."

"I just wanna talk to him."

"When he gets this angry, space is all he needs. Give him time."

"But how is he mad when…"

"The same way you were mad when you knew he was still sleeping with Ronny. The difference is, he never stopped messing with her and you knew it. He may not have informed anyone of what you two had going on but he's been real with you from the start."

"I'm not wrong."

"If you felt you weren't wrong, then you weren't. But I am going to ask you this." I heard the door shut and looked behind to see her in the driver's side.

"If you weren't wrong, why are you so upset?"

"Because he had no right to send y'all where I was and beat Marcus up. We're not together."

"You're a grown woman and can do what you want but why did you jump in bed with dude?" She didn't say a word.

"Another thing Khloe."

"What?"

"Why do you care what he thinks and why haven't you left?" She pulled off without saying a word. I never looked at her and passed him the small portion of the blunt when he jumped back in the car.

"Thanks for intervening. Shit would've went left."

"Y'all niggas need to get it together."

"I was willing to go the distance but if revenge is what she does every time she's mad, I'll pass. She can continue being there for Raina and I'll keep it moving. I don't need the extra drama.

****

BOOM! I pounded on the door and waited for someone to answer.

"Ryan, what's going on?" Ms. Singer, Veronica's mom asked as my crew ran through her house.

"Check everywhere. Under beds, closets, showers, trapped doors and anywhere you think the bitch could be hiding."

"Oh my God, what did she do?" I sat down in a chair and stared at her. I wasn't mad at her but more mad at myself for not seeing her hurting my daughter. Granted, making her throwing up ain't as bad as suicide but it's all around fucked up.

"Where is she?"

"I don't know."

BOOM! BOOM! I heard and one of the guys came down with some papers.

"What was the noise?"

"Oh, there was a small door in the room and we couldn't open it, so we knocked it off the hinges." He shrugged his shoulders. I took the papers out his hand and her mom seemed nervous about me reading them, which only made me read them faster.

Veronica Singer (AKA Bridget Smalls) is a threat to herself and anyone around her. She is currently on medication for depression and suicide. She should not be allowed within fifty feet of any child and is placed on Tier 2 of the sex offender list. Anything after that couldn't be read because I had her mother up in the air, by the throat.

"What the fuck is this?" She had tears rolling down her face.

"Bro, she can't talk because her face is turning blue." I dropped her and listened to her body slam into the floor. I snatched the papers off the table.

"What…The…Fuck…Is…This?" I mushed them in her face.

"Please. I told her to tell you."

"Tell me what?"

"Veronica has been dealing with depression and tried to kill herself a few times."

"I don't give a fuck about her dying. I wanna know what the hell this sex offender shit is. Was she raping little boys?"

"Ryan, please." I felt bad but only for a second because she's always been nice to me.

"Tell me right fucking now." I grabbed her by the shirt and lifted her off the floor. I never disrespected adults but this is an exception.

"Veronica was molested when she was young." Waleed came walking through the door as she started to tell me the story.

"What happened?" He was late due to the doctors' appointment him and Luna had this morning. I told him to hold on and listen.

"She told me but I didn't believe her until she tried to take her life more than once."

"Ok. What else?" I knew it was a lot more to this story.

"Well, the person was arrested and went to jail. Fast forward to maybe ten years ago, Veronica was caught doing the same thing to someone else's child. The cops arrested her and she spent five years behind bars. She came home on medication and had to register as a sex offender for the rest of her life. I had Veronica, I mean Bridget change her name for her own protection and to start a new life."

"Hold up. She was raping little boys?" Waleed asked the same question I did. The look on Ms. Singer's face hit me like a ton of bricks. She didn't even have to say it, for me to know what was about to leave her mouth.

"No. She was molesting little girls."

"POW! POW! POW POW! I shot her over and over. Waleed took the gun out my hand.

"What happened?" The other guys came in the house and saw Ms. Singer's body slumped over and her head blown off. Waleed stared at me.

"The bitch should've made her daughter tell me." I hauled ass outta there and sped to Khloe's fathers house, which is where Raina was. I banged on the door until Khloe's dad came to the door.

"Hey Mr. Banks. Is Raina here?"

"Yea. Her and Khloe are out back. Is everything ok?" He closed the door. I didn't mean to ignore him but I needed to see my daughter.

106

Khloe

"Not right now." I told Ryan who walked in the backyard with a hateful look on his face. This is the first time, we've seen one another since he had Marcus shot up, over a week ago. He still allowed me to spend time with Raina, who's' been here just about everyday. She's even been back and forth to the hospital with me. I meant what I said about her not leaving my sight. If I couldn't keep her, my father would and I had to make sure she was comfortable with that. After all she's been through, I'd hate for her to be put in any similar situations.

"We're over Khloe so you don't have to worry about that. Come here Raina." I have to admit, him saying that stung. I was still in love with him and thought he wanted to talk about us but hearing him say we were over, pushed the thought right out my head.

"Daddy, is everything ok?" She wrapped the towel around her. We were in the pool on those rafts you lie down on.

"Everything's good but I need to talk to you." She wrapped her hair in a ponytail and sat next to him. I grabbed my towel and did the same after asking if he were ok with me staying. If he said no, I would've went in the house and listened from the door anyway. It's probably why he said yes.

"I'm gonna ask you something and no matter how hard its going to be for me to hear, I need you to be truthful, ok?" She nodded and let the tears fall. Its like she knew what her dad was going to ask, where my dumb ass had no idea. Did she do something with his mom, that she never mentioned?

"Raina, did..." I could hear his hesitation.

"Did ummmm... Shit, I don't even know how to ask." He was rubbing his hands on the shorts he wore.

"Are you ok Ryan?"

"Nah, I'm not. Just tryna figure out how to word this shit." He stood up and started pacing. Raina came and sat closer to me.

"Ryan, whatever it is, just say it. You're making her nervous." He stopped and stared.

"Did Veronica touch you inappropriately at anytime?" My mouth hit the floor. I knew someone touched her but she never said who. Then each time we were about to speak on it, something came up. Honestly, I assumed it was a man because she never specified if it were a woman or not.

"Yes." I covered my mouth.

"How many times?" He asked and we both waited for her to answer. I knew it was three years but I'm not sure how many times. It could've been once a year but whatever it was, we were both abut to find out.

"A lot."

"What's a lot?"

"Its been happening for three years." Ryan had her stand and hugged her tight. After a few minutes, he looked at her.

"I'm so fucking sorry Raina. How could I not know?" His eyes were watery and regret washed all over his face.

"Its not your fault daddy. I didn't tell you and…" Raina was tryna explain but his anger got the best of him and he wasn't tryna hear anything she said. I saw murder in his eyes and knew once he found Veronica it was over.

"It is my fault. I should've known and killed her. FUCK!!!!" He started flipping the patio chairs, table and anything else in his way.

"DADDY, STOP!" Raina went over to him and I noticed his gun on the side and grabbed her back. I know he would never hurt her but accidents happen.

"Ms. K, it's not his fault. She said if I told, she'd kill him and my nana. I didn't want to lose him too. Daddy, please stop. Ms. K, please make him stop." She was hysterical crying. I tried my best to calm her but with him flipping out, I couldn't.

"What's going on?" My dad opened the sliding door and glanced around. Shit, was everywhere, and Raina was upset so I can see why he was concerned.

"Can you take her inside?"

"I love you daddy." She gave him a hug and stood on her tippy toes to kiss his cheek.

"Raina, he's gonna be fine. Go change and order some lunch." She wiped her eyes, stared at her dad one more time and went in the house. I waited until she walked away and my dad stood there.

"Its ok daddy." He nodded and went back in the living room. I started picking the chairs up and whatever else he tossed and waited for him to get off the phone.

"I DON'T GIVE A FUCK IF YOU NEED A GOT DAMN BLOODHOUND TO FIND HER. I WANT HER IN FRONT OF ME ASAP." He tossed the phone across the lawn and placed his hands on top of his head. I wanted to wrap my arms around him but with what he said about us not being together, stopped me. I walked around and stood in front of him. He had tears falling down his face.

"How did I miss that shit K? I was always home and she never seemed to be out of it, until recently."

"Ryan."

"Do you know I've left her home alone with Veronica; well Bridget? Was she doing this the entire time? FUCK!" I wiped his tears.

"Who the hell is Bridget?"

"Oh, that's Veronica's real name."

"Now, I'm confused."

"Evidently the bitch has a history of doing this shit and was placed on the sex offender list. Don't ask me how she was able to get her name changed, but she did. Her mom thought it was best to get a fresh start under an alias." He put his hands up using quotations.

"Oh my God."

"Khloe, before I even made it official with her, I had her checked out thoroughly. Nowhere in her file did it say anything about it. Its like her mom or someone had the shit hidden and if you didn't know, you wouldn't find it."

"That's crazy." I was in shock listening to him.

"I left the streets alone so I could spend more time with Raina. Yea, I still worked at the funeral home and dabbled in some shit, here and there but I was always around. Why didn't she tell me? I would've believed her." I grabbed his hand and took him to sit down. I sat on his lap and he wrapped his arms around me.

"Ryan, she doesn't blame you. There's no way, you could've known."

"Did she tell you?" My heart started beating fast when he asked but I had to tell him the truth.

"Yes and no." I felt him remove his arms.

"The first time she went in the hospital and I went to visit the next day, I asked and she told me yes."

"And you didn't say anything." He basically pushed me off.

"Ryan, she refused to tell me who the person was. Luna and I were ready to find the person and beat them up. She begged me not to and I told her there's no way I could hold it in. When you came from the police station, I told her to tell you. Then, when my mother was attacked and we found her again, I was going to tell you but my mother was rushed to the hospital." I made him look at me.

"I had every intention to tell you and things kept popping up and made me stop. The time I was finally going to tell you, Raina jumped out the car and stopped me. Do you remember? She said, Ms. K won't tell you because I asked her not to." He nodded.

"Ryan, if I told you in front of her she would've lost her trust in me and we would've never gotten as far as we did."

"You should've told me."

"I'm sorry and had I known who the person was, I would have, after I killed her myself." I told him and went towards the door.

"I just don't understand how anyone can do something like this to a kid." I stopped and turned around.

"She's sick Ryan and played off the death of her mother. The bitch knew saying those things would scare her. But what you can't do, is blame yourself."

"But she needed me and I wasn't there." I could see how bad he was fighting himself on not knowing.

"You were there Ryan. She probably feels as long as your alive, she'd take it."

"But then she tried to take her life."

"I spoke with her about the first time, and she said it was the only way to escape Veronica but the second time…" I was about to tell him, she never got around to telling me but she came out and answered.

"The second time she did it." Raina came out dressed in shorts and a t-shirt.

"What do you mean?" We both asked at the same time.

She went on to tell us, after she touched her in my house, Veronica found a belt and took her in the bathroom. She punched her in the stomach a few times for not listening and tied it around her throat and shower rod. The reason she didn't watch her die is because I came home and she heard me calling for her. I have no idea how she escaped with me there but she did.

"I have to find her." He tried to storm off but I stopped him.

"Not today."

"What you mean, not today. That bitch needs to fucking die."

"You're so right but Raina needs you. Stay here and be with her." He looked behind him and Raina was sitting there crying. He ran over to her and I left them alone. My dad asked me what was going on and after I told him, he was ready to find Veronica himself and kill her. I had no doubt in my mind that Ryan is going to do just that.

****

"I'm leaving Raina. You better hurry up." I told her on my way down the steps. She's been here every day and refuses to go home or her nana's. Ryan was here as well and scared to leave her because he felt like it would be neglecting her. I had to get Waleed to make him come over and take him out somewhere this morning. He was driving both of us crazy. Once Raina came down the steps, I locked up and we left.

"What up heffa and Raina, I'm still waiting on my damn lasagna." Luna hopped in the car. We were going to breakfast after dropping her off at school.

"Aunt Luna, you have to buy the stuff. I'm broke."

"Lies you tell."

"I am."

"Your father has money and I know this tight ho, got money." I noticed Raina look up from the rearview mirror.

"Bitch, I ain't no ho."

"You lucky she's in the back, otherwise; I'd call you out." I gave her the finger and you could hear Raina laughing.

"Here we are." I parked in front of the school and she sat there. Luna and I looked at her and fear was on her face.

"What's wrong?" She pointed at some kids.

"Ok. Did they do something to you?"

"They bother me everyday."

"SAY WHAT?" Luna shouted and took her seatbelt off.

"They say I'm dirty and sleep with all the middle school boys." Her head was down in embarrassment.

"You're only in the seventh grade." I told her.

"I know. But they still say it. They say, my mom is happy to be dead because her daughter is a loser and.-" I didn't even let her finish.

"You said this is everyday?" I opened my car door and didn't even have to look and know Luna was behind me. I had Raina get out and she walked with her head down next to me.

"Lift your head up. Always look your haters in the eye."

"HEY!" I shouted and the kids turned around. It was a little boy and two girls who were skinny and probably stuck up.

"What the fuck your fat ass want?" One of them said and Lord knows I wanted to smack fire from her ass. I've been working on not hitting kids though.

"Oh shit." I heard some kid say and outta nowhere, it was mad kids around us.

"What's y'all name?"

"Why?"

"Just tell me your name." The one speaking placed her hand on her hip and rolled her eyes.

"I'm Giselle, this is Brea and he's Nate." She pointed to who, was who. I stared at each of them and noticed the expensive clothes and sneakers they were rocking. Raina wore all up to date stuff too, so I wondered why they were bothering her. Most of the time, bullies bothered people who had nothing. Well, I thought they did.

"I wanna know why you're bullying Raina?" I hated to use the word but from what Raina described, its exactly what they were doing.

"Ain't nobody bullying her fat ass." Luna snatched the little girl up by the shirt.

"That is bullying right there motherfucker. You calling her names and shit, ain't cool."

"Get the fuck off me." Brea said and tried to pry Luna's hands off.

"Make me. You tough bitch. Make me." Luna had the girl by her hair now and pushed her to the ground. The kids started laughing but the other two weren't saying shit.

"You two. What's up?"

"You can't touch us." Giselle said as if I gave a fuck about the attitude she was giving me.

"Why not?" I mushed her in the face and the boy stood off to the side.

"I'm telling my mother. How the fuck you fat bitches up here starting with kids anyway?" I smacked the fuck outta her.

"Oooooh." You heard all the kids instigating, like they normally do when someone is about to fight.

"Yooooo, she just smacked the shit outta you." I heard a boy yell.

"Bitch, get yo momma, yo daddy, uncles, aunts and whoever else. I'll stand right here and wait." I told her and passed her my phone but she pushed it away. I glanced over at Luna and she had the girl on the ground with her foot on her back.

"Fuck you." The minute she said that, I popped her over and over in the mouth and didn't stop until I saw some of the teachers coming in our direction. By that time, her mouth was busted. I gave zero fucks because these kids were disrespectful as hell but they gonna learn today.

"Excuse me. What are you doing to these kids?" Some woman came over. She was dark skinned and looked to be about the same weight as me.

"Oh I'm bullying them, like they've been doing my stepdaughter." I stood there waiting ti hear what she had to say but the next thing out her mouth had me floored.

"What? I told you kids a hundred times to leave her alone."

"You knew?" I pushed the little girl on the ground and dared her to get up. I went in the lady's face and was flabbergasted when she claimed to be the principal.

"You knew they were doing this and didn't contact her father?"

"Well, I thought they would stop."

"Beat her ass Khloe." Luna said and the woman looked scared as hell. I pulled her over to the side.

"Do you have any idea what Raina has gone through because of your stupidity?" She didn't say anything.

"DO YOU?" She jumped.

"Stay yo ass on the ground." Luna told both girls who didn't move.

"I was going to mention it to her father if it happened again."

"AGAIN! BITCH IT NEVER SHOULDVE HAPPENED AFTER THE FIRST TIME." She agreed and after ripping her a new asshole in front of what now seemed to be half the school, I walked back over to the kids who we had stand up.

"If Raina comes home today or any other day saying you even said hello to her, I'm gonna beat your ass like a bitch off the street. I don't give a fuck how old you are either. As you can see, we'll go to war for her so I better not hear anything else. Do I make myself clear?" I had the little girl jacked up in front of the tree.

"Yes." She had tears coming down her face.

"Guess yo ass ain't so tough now. Get yo bitch ass out my face before I smack you again." I let go and pushed her in the direction of the school.

"And you." I pointed to the boy.

"Why in the fuck are you bothering little girls?"

"Man, my older cousin paid us to do it." I looked at Luna.

"Nate, you're not supposed to tell."

"Fuck that. If these two ladies beat y'all ass, I'm not gonna wait for their niggas to come get me. Especially; her father. I'm good." The shit that come outta these kids mouths.

"If you know about her father why do this shit to her?"

"We've been doing this for a while and I didn't think she would tell." He shrugged his shoulders.

"Who is your older cousin?"

"Veronica. She said fuck with Raina everyday."

"And how much did she pay you?" Luna asked them.

"Twenty dollars." I shouted.

"That's it? Nigga, you been bothering her for that little bit of money? You could've charged at least a hundred each. Y'all should be ashamed of yourselves for even accepting that little bit of money." I smacked Luna on the arm.

"Where is Veronica?" I was ready to find and kill her or at least beat her ass real bad.

"I don't know. She was staying with her mom, and at my house but we haven't seen her in a week." Nate told us.

"Do me a favor and tell her the next time you see her, that Khloe Banks is coming for her." He nodded and walked inside. The principal was standing there looking dumb as fuck and so were the other teachers. I heard sirens in the distance, which let me know someone called the cops.

123

"Go ahead Raina." She smiled and gave both Luna and I a hug. We watched her walk in and stayed there until the cops came. Believe it or not, neither one of us were worried. I'd do the shit again for Raina or any other kid being bullied everyday. I don't know what's wrong with these bad ass kids now a days, but they got the right fucking one.

Luna

I leaned on the car listening to this dumb ass principle tell the cops how we were beating on some kids. Yet; she left out her not informing Raina's father about the bullying and abuse those kids did to her. I wasn't worried because my dad's lawyer was on his way and so was Waleed. He called to see why I wasn't at the diner eating with Khloe like I told him I would be. Yea, he became a stalker now that I'm pregnant but more because Oscar and Julie are still lurking and he's concerned.

"Who put their hands on my daughter?" Some woman yelled and Khloe and I turned around to see Veronica and another lady. The cops weren't fast enough for Khloe. She ran up on Veronica and started beating the hell outta her. The other chick tried to jump in and I caught her in the exact spot to knock her out. She was sleep on the ground.

"Ok Khloe." Waleed said and lifted her up.

"GET OFF ME WALEED! IM GONNA FUCKING KILL HER!" She was shouting and trying her hardest to get back over there.

"Calm your hostile ass down. Risky may not put his hands on you but I'll choke the shit outta you." He started laughing and I punched him in the stomach.

"Luna I'ma fuck yo ass up later."

"Yea ok. Don't be coming for her. You know damn well that bitch deserved it." We all looked and she was gone.

"Where the fuck is she?" We knew she couldn't get in the school so she must've ran.

"We have to go. I slammed her head on the ground a few times. She has to be dizzy or have a concussion, which means she didn't get far."

"Let's go." We started to walf off.

"You're not going anywhere." Two cops came over and placed handcuffs on us.

"Yo, What the fuck?" Waleed has a snarl on his face.

"These two women are charged with child abuse, endangering the welfare of a child and a list of other charges."

"If that's the case, this woman also needs to be arrested for allowing children to bully my niece and harass her everyday. My brother is meeting us down at the station to press charges on the kids too."

"They're kids. They fight all the time." The bitch had the nerve to say.

"Which is why your dumb ass needs to be fired. You knew all this was going on and did nothing." Waleed said. I filled him on everything before he got there and he was fired up because of what she allowed to go on in the school.

"Is that true? Did you know the kids were fighting his niece and didn't do anything?" When she started stuttering another cop placed her in cuffs too. They didn't take bullying lightly anymore and once the cops found out she knew, she was being charged with the same thing. The only difference is we don't work here.

"Looks like we'll be cell mates and you're gonna lose your job. I'm posting it all over social media." I could get very petty at times.

"Why are you doing this?" She asked as they walked her past the cop car we were in.

"Because you failed all those kids." I turned around and saw Khloe crying. We were in the same car.

"What's wrong?"

"I let Veronica get away."

"She's not gonna get far K." I hope she didn't anyway.

"I had her Luna. She was right there and now she's in the wind."

"Risky's gonna find her."

"I hope so."

"Bitch, you pregnant?" I asked because she was doing too much crying for me.

"HELL NO!"

"Why you say it like that?" Everyone was well aware of how much she loved him so even if she were pregnant, none of us would be surprised.

"I knew he was tryna get me pregnant Luna and started using those diaphragm things. You know in case the guy doesn't wear a condom, I'd still be protected. And the days he caught me off guard, I'd take a plan b pill." My mouth dropped.

"I know it's not good to take too many but I also didn't want a man trapping me so I didn't sleep with anyone else." The cop got in the car and pulled off.

"But you're in love with him."

"I am but I love myself more. Luna, he said he felt the same and I believe him but until he actually shows me the change, we can't be together and I'm not pushing no kid out."

"Wait! So you're really done with him?"

"As hard as it is for me to say, yes I am." I nodded my head and she rested her head on my shoulder. I can see the love displayed on her face, however; I totally agree with her about him showing and proving. Too much has happened for him not to.

****

"I'm here for Khloe Banks." We heard and turned around. Risky stood there talking to the lady as we sat at one of the desks telling the two lady cops what happened. They were cracking up and said those kids deserved to get their ass beat for bullying somebody.

We sat there talking to them for a good twenty minutes before my lawyer came strolling in demanding to speak with the captain. Loud ass Waleed walked in behind him and asked for the bathroom and then disappeared down the hall, in search for some damn vending machines. Talking about me being here had him stressed out so he smoked on the way and now he's hungry. I swear the shit I put up with regarding him, has me asking myself how am I even with him.

"I'm right here Ryan." Khloe stood and he tried to get in but the bottom half of the door was locked. You know the kind where you can open the top and leave the bottom one closed? Its like that. One of the officers opened the door and he walked over to her.

"Why y'all beating up kids?" He couldn't contain his laugh either.

"Fuck them little crumb snatchers. They should've never bothered Raina." He stood there staring at Khloe, and me and the two cops stood there, staring at him.

"You love my daughter?"

"Yup and if you don't like it too bad."

"Nah, I love it." He placed a kiss on her cheek and I could tell Khloe wanted more but he kept it strictly on a friend level.

"Ummm, can you take me to get my car?" I think she was embarrassed.

"Yea, come on. You need a ride too?" He looked me up and down.

"No, I don't. My man here and why you giving me the once over?"

"Because I need to know why yo ass, putting your feet on kids back?" He showed me a video of us at the school. The kids posted it n Snap Chat and Raina sent it to him.

"What the fuck ever. I bet those bitches don't say two fucking words to Raina again." Khloe and I slapped hands.

"Get yo convict ass in the truck. Both of y'all crazy." He held the door for K and walked out behind her. If those two don't hurry up and get I together, I'm gonna scream.

"YO! CAN MY GIRL GO HOME YET? I NEED TO LET THIS NUT OUT! Y'ALL GOT ME STRESSED THE FUCK OUT." I put my head down.

"Is he like this every day?" One of the cops asked as she continued laughing.

"ALL THE TIME!" I shook my head and made my way to the door.

"About damn time." He said and hopped on the passenger's side and told me to drive because he was too high. I can't wait to get his annoying ass home.

****

"Luna don't play with me. You better suck my babies out." We ended up fucking as soon as we got home just like he wanted.

"Mmmmm, well cum for me then." I was being extra nasty with Waleed but before we had sex I told him I wasn't swallowing.

"I swear if you get up. Fuckkkkk!" He moaned out and shot every seed down my throat. I was gonna get up but didn't feel like arguing over it. He was spoiled as hell when it came to sex with me. I should've never given him all I had because he expects it every time.

"You know how to suck some dick don't you? Come here." I climbed on top and rested my pussy on his face. In the beginning, I was nervous as hell to do this because of my weight but he never took no for an answer. Shit, I was shocked he could even lift me but he did with no complaints.

"Baby, yes. Oh fuck yes." My juices dripped down his face and I felt his tongue cleaning me up

"You love me Luna?" He asked as I moved off.

"I don't know anymore." He pinched my leg.

"Ok. Ok. I love you. I love you a whole lot." He placed kisses on my belly.

"Good because I'm gonna kill Oscar and Julie."

"Huh?" He never answered because his dick was inside shifting my uterus and anything else he could touch.

Veronica

"Who are those bitches?" My cousin Ashley asked when she got home. After the fat bitch basically beat my ass; I jumped up and ran. My head was dizzy and blood leaked down behind my ear but I got my ass outta there. If I didn't know any better I'd say she was tryna kill me.

"That's some bitch Risky sleeping with." I grabbed the ice cube tray out the fridge, dumped some in a Ziploc bag, and placed it on the back of my head.

"Nah. Risky ain't sleeping with no fat chick." She said texting way on her phone. It was probably some of her home girls from around the way. My cousin Ashley was from the ghetto, acted ghetto and would get ghetto, any and everywhere. I hated to be around her and them but right now I needed her because I was too scared to be out alone. I knew after the shit I pulled with Khloe catching me fucking Risky, she'd be on the lookout for me and I was right.

"That's what I said. Shit, the day I caught him at her house he said fucking fat bitches ain't his thing. She heard him, cried and threw all his stuff out. But that's not the kicker." My cousin stared at me.

"The kicker is him showing emotion for her. It's like he felt bad for letting her hear him say it. He was hurting for her."

"I know you lying." She seemed as shocked as I was. We all know the type of man he is so hearing that he's with a fat chick, seems unbelievable.

"Is he in love with her?"

"I don't know." I answered truthfully because I didn't.

"What you doing about it? And where those bitches stay? We need to go there."

"For what? Them to beat us up again?" She sucked her teeth. As I got up to run, this bitch was on the ground dead sleep and I left her ass right there. No need for both of us to be out cold. Now she asking where they live, like she gonna really do something. I rolled my eyes and looked down at my phone. There was a message from Raina asking me to meet her in a private place. It's a little out the blue but I miss her. I sent a

135

text telling her we could meet in a few days. I had to figure out my next move and get rid of this headache. I'm sure she gave me a concussion but it would be dumb to go to the hospital. I'm not sure if Risky is looking for me or not but I'm not taking chances.

"What happened at school?" Ashley snapped at her daughter Giselle, who walked in with her sister Brea and our other cousin, Nate. We were all related but those fuckers bad as hell. I mean they disrespectful as fuck and will curse out anyone. I wonder if that's the reason Khloe and Luna laid hands on them.

I wasn't surprised when Giselle sent a text saying some ladies were up there tryna fight them. Those heffa's were grown as hell and always in some shit. I guess, the apple don't fall far from the tree.

"Those two ladies smacked us and threw us on the ground." Brea had her hands on her hip. This the shit I'm talking about. She ain't fucking grown.

"And boy what did you do?"

"Not a damn thing. Ma, that's Risky's daughter and I'm not bothering her anymore." I gave him a weird look. How did he knew she was Risky's daughter because I never told him? Everyone feared him, even the kids which is the exact reason I didn't tell them who she was.

"How did you know who she was?" I asked to feed my curiosity.

"Once, I saw the lady get out the car, I knew."

"And how is that?"

"Raina has a photo of them on her Instagram." He showed it to us and I'll be damned. It was a photo with the three of them at some house watching television. Khloe was on one side of Raina and Risky was on the other. He showed me one more and it was Risky standing behind her in what seems to be the hospital and whispering in her ear or some shit. I was pissed. Was he showing her off now? When did he fall for fat girls?

"Why were you bothering her anyway?" Ashley asked and I looked at them.

"Veronica paid us $20 to do it."

"You a snitch Giselle?" I said and Ashley gave me a weird look.

"Really?" I shrugged my shoulders and called the other two a snitch as well.

"I'll deal with y'all later. Let me talk to Veronica real quick." Giselle stuck her middle finger up, Brea rolled her eyes at me and Nate bid me farewell. Talking about, I'm gonna die when Risky finds out what I had them doing.

"I don't even wanna talk about the shit you had the kids doing right now but we will later." I ignored her and continued scrolling on my Instagram.

"We need to find these bitches and show them who they fucking with." I busted out laughing. My cousin ain't tough at all. She got the nerve to be pacing the floor like she really gonna whoop some ass.

"Can you take me to my mother's?"

"For what? We rolling out to find those chicks."

"Fine! I'll go but I need to get something from my mother's house." She finally gave in and when her ghetto ass friend came, we were all two cars deep rolling out.

138

"I'll be right out." I hopped out the car, ran in the house and up the steps without stopping to speak to my mom. If I did, she'd most likely bitch about me telling Risky. To be honest, there's no need now that we're not together.

"What the hell?" I opened the door to my room and it looked as if a tornado hit it. Shit was everywhere and the little door where I kept important papers was off he hinges. It was a tiny crawl space like door, and my mom had me keep anything important in there.

I looked inside and the papers were gone. I searched my entire room tryna find them but it was no use. It made me wonder who the hell she allowed in here to do it because I know, she didn't. After looking in her bedroom and not finding her, I went downstairs only to find her body laid out on the floor with her face unrecognizable. I only knew it was her because of the pajamas she wore.

"Yo, Veronica lets go." I heard and slid down the wall crying. Who would kill my mom and in such a violent way?

"Oh my God! What happened?" Ashley picked the house phone up and dialed 911 with tears falling down her

139

eyes too. She loved my mom like her own and once she hung up, sat there crying with me.

When the cops arrived, they helped us stand and asked us to go outside because it was a crime scene. I bent down to pick up the papers off the floor and sure enough, they were the ones I'd tried to keep hidden. Ashley asked me what they were and I just said, my birth certificate and other important papers. She never asked to see them and went out the door with me. Neighbors and people riding by were staring extremely hard and it only pissed me off.

"When we find out who did this, we're gonna kill them." I gave my cousin a fake smile because I knew she was just talking.

The cops had us there for hours asking questions about who would wanna hurt my mother and if she had enemies. You know the regular dumb questions they ask. Afterwards, I went straight to Ashley's house and took my ass to bed. Whoever did this is gonna pay dearly, I can promise you that.

Risky

"Raina baby, where are you?" I cringed listening to Veronica call out for my daughter. Waleed looked at me shaking his head.

It had been a couple of weeks since her mom died and it took a very long time to find her. The dumb bitch didn't even attend her own mothers' funeral because word in the street was that she was scared of running into me. Evidently, she told people we broke up and I was stalking her to stay with me. *Go figure!*

We listened to her call out for Raina a few more times as she went upstirs, and room to room. I texted her from Raina's phone and told her to meet at one of Waleed's trap houses. It was furnished and decorated like someone actually lived here. It's supposed to look that way and since this dumb bitch can't tell the difference, it's definitely a good cover up.

I heard her coming towards the kitchen and felt my leg shaking. I was ready to kill her on the spot but Khloe told me whenever I find her to ask why she did it first. Otherwise; it would be on my mind and if she's dead I could never ask.

Thinking about Khloe made me realize how good of a woman she really is. She took a liking to Raina before knowing I was her father and has been by my side ever since, even when we're not speaking. Am I mad she slept with dude? Hell yea! I also know she's hurt for the way I treated her. I did wanna make shit up to her but she jumped in bed with someone else and Sandy is occupying my time now.

"What up Ronny?" She froze and looked around the kitchen. It was Waleed, and the people who are gonna get rid of her when I'm done. See, they all love Raina and once they heard what she did, they insisted on being here.

"Ummm, what are you doing here?" I stood.

"Expecting someone else?" I moved closer and ran my hand down her exposed arm.

"Raina text me something was wrong so I ran over to make sure she's ok." She was lying her ass off because that's not what I said in the messages. At first, she wouldn't come and it took a lot of convincing but she finally gave in.

"Oh. Ok." Is all I said and stared at her.

"Risky we may not be together but I still love her like my own child." I heard one of the guys suck their teeth.

"And Raina looked at you as a mother figure but answer me this." It seemed as if she were becoming comfortable.

"You say she's like a daughter to you but you were molesting her."

"Risky."

"Why were you touching my daughter? You made her do things to you and herself. Then she tried to kill herself in order to keep you from bothering her. Let's not forget to mention the kids you had bullying her at school and the fact you never told me who you really were, Bridget." Her mouth dropped to the floor.

"Did you kill my mother?"

"I sure did and I'm gonna kill you too. I just need a little more information from you first." I gave her a fake smile and she tried to back out the kitchen but Waleed was blocking the doorway.

"What? You didn't think I'd find out who you were?" I started pacing back and forth to try and relax but each second passing and I looked at her, it became harder.

"Granted it took a while but I know now. How could you do that to Raina after everything she been through with her mom and…"

"I'm in love with her." I stopped and all the guys looked at her.

"What the fuck did you just say?"

"I don't know why I'm like this and if I could take back everything I would but I can't. My aunt did it to me for so long and got away with it, I thought I would too. But Raina and I are in love and…"

"Are you serious right now? My niece is twelve fucking years old and from what we hear, you've been doing this for three years." Waleed was beyond pissed. Hell, we all were.

"HOW THE FUCK ARE YOU IN LOVE WITH MY DAUGHTER?" I screamed out.

144

"I'm sorry." I had my hand behind her head and banged her face into the wall. I heard her nose crack.

"Sorry huh?" I kicked her in the stomach over and over. Waleed had to pull me off. She was slumped over on the ground.

"Pass me the ax." Waleed handed it to me and Veronica's eyes grew big.

"Didn't your momma ever teach you not to touch things that don't belong to you?" I lifted the ax, brought it down and chopped both of her hands off. She screamed.

"I was gonna shoot you but then there would've been no suffering and I think you deserve to suffer." I wanted to hang her by the ceiling but changed my mind because she'd die faster. Bad enough her hands were on the ground and blood was gushing out like a waterfall. Instead, I chopped off both of her feet and continued on the rest of her until there was no more screaming or connected body parts. I chopped that bitch up like food and the floor was the cutting board. She fucked with the wrong nigga.

"She's dead man." Waleed took the ax.

145

"Good. Now Raina can sleep better. Dumb bitch." I kicked one of her hands across the kitchen floor and everyone jumped.

"See y'all later." One of them stood in front of the door.

"Clean yourself up first." I stepped back and went in the downstairs bathroom. I had blood on my clothes, face and in my hair. After wiping down as much as I could and walked out, the smell of gasoline overtook the entire house and it was up in flames by the time, I sat in my car.

"Go tell Raina so she can relax." I nodded and hopped in the car with Waleed. My daughter was gonna be happy and afterwards I would be too. Especially, once I release this nut.

****

"How do you feel hearing the woman won't bother you anymore?" Ms. Preston asked Raina who appeared to be more into her phone. I took it and made her answer. Raina didn't know what exactly happened to Veronica but if I told her not to ever worry about something, she already knew I wasn't lying. My daughter's not naïve to the street gossip but she doesn't ask questions either.

"I'm happy my dad took care of it. The nightmares stopped and…" Just as she said that someone knocked on the door. Ms. Preston walked over and opened it.

"Am I on time?" I heard her voice and turned around to see Khloe standing there looking fucking gorgeous.

She had on a pair of fitted jeans with some sandals, to show off her pretty feet. The shit she had on exposed some of her cleavage and I couldn't help but reminisce on sucking on her titties. Her hair was done and she smelled good as hell. This is my first time seeing her since killing Veronica and that was a few weeks ago.

Raina was staying with me at my mom's because she refused to live in that house of horrors, as she put it and I didn't blame her. She and I have been house hunting but so far there's nothing she approved of. As far as Khloe goes, she usually picks her up when I'm gone and the same goes when she's dropping her off.

"I'm sorry, who are you?" The doctor asked with a hint of sarcasm.

"Ms. K. You made it." Raina ran over to her. I was shocked to see her because this meeting was supposed to take place weeks ago.

"Oh you're Ms. K." The therapist reached out and shook her hand.

"I am. Can I come in?" Before Ms. Preston could answer, Raina had already led her inside. The smile on my daughter face always made me happy. I licked my lips when Khloe leaned over to pick up her phone that dropped. I could see straight down her shirt.

"Ok then. Shall we?" Ms. Preston started asking Khloe questions about the situation with Raina and then, she went to ask some that I felt were inappropriate. I stopped Khloe from answering the ones pertaining to me because it wasn't her business and had nothing to do with the therapy session.

"Can we go now daddy?" Raina asked as I stood there staring at Khloe, who was getting ready to knock the hell outta Ms. Preston.

"Yea. Go wait in the hallway and don't move." She grabbed Khloe's hand and both of them left the room. Once they closed the door I went in on her.

"Yo, What the fuck is wrong with you?" She walked around her desk.

"That woman wants you." I had to laugh because if she only knew.

"That has nothing to do with therapy for my daughter. Then you asking crazy questions in front of Raina." She fell back in the chair.

"I'm sorry. It's just that over the last two weeks, I've started catching feelings. I don't want anyone to interfere in what we're building." *Building?* This bitch barely knows me and we building already.

After the suicide attempt with Raina, she stayed in touch. I never called her and most of the time, had to call her back. Two weeks ago, we ran into one another and I promised to call her. Anyway, we went out to eat and been kicking it ever since. It's unprofessional as hell to date the guy, whose daughter you're helping but Sandy is bad as hell. She reminded

149

me of Nelly's girlfriend and her sex is pretty good. Oh yea, I fucked her after the first date. I had to know if the pussy was worth anything.

"Sandy look." She came over to me and wrapped her arms on my neck and I let my hands rest on her ass.

"Khloe and my daughter are very close and I'm letting you know, that no woman is going to ruin what they have."

"I'm not trying to baby. Raina has gone through a lot and it's good to have a mother figure around, regardless if she's a bigger woman and doesn't resemble her mom."

"Say what?" I pushed her off.

"Don't you want a woman she can relate more too?"

"A woman's weight has nothing to do with helping a man raise his kid. And why the fuck would I want someone who resembled her mom?"

"I didn't mean it in a bad way." She must've noticed how angry I was because her hands were under my shirt and she was rubbing my chest.

"Ryan, I'm gonna.-" Khloe says barging in the office. My body was halfway turned so she couldn't see exactly what Sandy was doing but you could tell something was going on.

"You can come in Ms. K. My man was just about to come out."

"Your man?" I had to look at her too. Yea, we fucking but we ain't no couple.

"Khloe?" She put her hand up. I could see how upset she was.

"It's ok Ryan." I turned all the way around and Sandy wrapped her arms on my waist. Her hands were dipping in and out the top of my jeans. We all knew she was doing it on purpose.

"I'll leave you alone." The way she said it sounded like it was forever. Sandy, may not have gotten it but I did.

"Wait!" I attempted to go after her but Sandy damn near had my dick in her hands. I turned around and fixed my clothes.

"Yo. We ain't no couple and that shit is childish as hell."

"I'm staking claim on you and whether we're a couple or not, you're the only man I'm sleeping with."

"Check this Sandy." I walked up on her and she backed up with a scared look on her face.

"You don't run shit and if you ever do that again, you'll regret it. Don't play games with me. I'll kill you, your whole family and do the funeral services with no guilt. Fuck with it, if you want." I turned to leave.

"Now you have a good day." I winked and slammed her door.

"I don't like her." Raina said when we started to leave.

"Why not?"

"She's sneaky daddy. I know she likes you but its something about her."

"What you know about being sneaky?" She raised her eyebrow.

"My bad. Where's Khloe?"

"She left upset. The doctor really pissed her off." I didn't respond to Raina and continued walking in silence. I knew K would be upset but as she keeps telling me, we're not together so why she mad?

I unlocked the door and both of us got in. Once I started the truck and backed out, I asked my daughter if she wanted to grab some food. Of course, she asked if we could invite Khloe. I told her no because its some things I wanted to speak with her about in private. I've been putting it off because I didn't know how to address it but there's no time like the present.

"Raina, put your phone away. I wanna talk to you." I told her and handed the lady back the menus. She did like I asked, opened the straw to sip her drink and waited. I couldn't help but see her mom and smiled.

"Why you smiling at me dad? That's weird?"

"I just wanna say a few things Raina and I don't want you to cut me off." She nodded and I blew my breath. It was hard to raise a girl to a woman and I'm happy Khloe, my mom and Luna's crazy ass are helping me but some things I have to deal with on my own.

"Raina, I am truly, truly sorry for everything that happened to you."

"Dad."

"Don't interrupt." She closed her mouth.

"I want you to know, I looked into Veronica's background before even allowing her to be around you. Nothing in there raised a red flag and there was a reason."

"It was?"

"Yea." I moved back a little and let the waitress place our appetizers on the table.

"Baby, what I'm about to tell you is gonna be a shock but just know, that had I known she would've been dead a long time ago."

"What is it?" She stared.

"The reason I couldn't find anything bad on her is because she had her name changed."

"Her name changed? What was it before?"

"Bridget Smalls." She busted out laughing, which made me do the same.

"Like Biggie Smalls? I know you have to be kidding me."

154

"No, that's her name." She poured ketchup on her fries that just came out and asked me if we could eat first and finish discussing it in the car. I agreed because not only was I hungry, I could tell in the beginning she was becoming upset. We sat there enjoying our food and talking about other things.

"Thank you and have a good day." The waitress handed me the check and went on about her way, as did we.

"We can finish now daddy." Raina said when we walked through the door of my mom's. I didn't think she wanted to finish so I never brought it back up. We both sat in the living room and I began speaking.

"I don't wanna bring too much up and make you upset but Raina she's done this before and I'm sorry for not protecting you better."

"Why did you keep sleeping with her, after you found out about her forcing me to throw up and me tryna kill myself?" And that's when she really broke down. I went over and hugged her. I thought she had an idea about me continuing to sleep with her but I wasn't sure until now.

155

"To be honest Raina, I still loved her and wanted it not to be true."

"Did you think I was lying?" I lifted her head up.

"Hell no! I believed you a hundred percent which is why I kept her away from you."

"But you were still with her."

"You're right and me still loving her should've never kept me going back, knowing what she did to you. It's not an excuse and if you don't ever forgive me for it, I totally understand." She wiped her eyes.

"Why did you stop sleeping with her?"

"Two reasons. One… is because after the last time we were together, I woke up the next day and thought about you and how it would make you feel, knowing I continued. It made me feel like shit for allowing her to stay in my life after she hurt you. And two… she wasn't worth losing my daughter's respect or love." I made her look at me.

"Raina, I was stupid for sticking around afterwards. You know I would do anything for you and I failed as a father for not getting rid of her sooner. Baby, I will apologize to you forever if you need me to. I am so fucking sorry." She wiped the tears now rolling down my face.

"I'm sorry for not telling you. I was so scared she'd try and get rid of you and nana, that I kept my mouth closed. Then the kids at school were bullying me so bad, I couldn't take it anymore and.-" I stopped her from speaking because she was so upset, she could barely speak.

"Raina, I need you to promise me if anything like this ever happens again, that you'll tell me. If not me, then Khloe, or Luna."

"I promise."

"Damn, I'm so fucking sorry you had to go through this and your mom is probably kicking my ass and stabbing me in heaven." We both busted out laughing.

"Yea, she probably is."

"Can we go visit her tomorrow?"

"You know we can go anytime you want."

"I know its just, I know you visit a lot by yourself, which is why I have nana take me. I know you like to have your own moment but I want us to go together more."

"How about from now on we go together. I've talked your moms ear off for years at that cemetery. She'd probably want us to come more at the same time anyway."

"Yea, you're right. Dad?"

"Yea." I had my chin on the top of her head as we stood there hugging.

"I forgive you." I moved her back.

"Thanks baby. You have no idea how happy you just made me."

"By saying I forgive you." She gave me a weird look.

"You'll learn in life that sometimes the smallest things a person does, and few words a person says, will mean more than material things."

"I love you Raina."

"I love you too dad." I kissed her cheek and the two of us went upstairs, changed in pajamas and laid on the couch for the rest of the day watching movies together. I planned on paying better attention to make sure this doesn't happen again. I never want my daughter hurting the way she was and if I have to stay by her side every day, then I'll do it.

Khloe

After walking out the therapist office, I was definitely in my feelings. Don't get me wrong, Risky had every right to move on but I guess seeing it made everything real, about us not being together. Did I think he'd still try after being mad? Of course, I did but the joke was on me. Especially; seeing her hands in his jeans. I could tell she did it on purpose and I also saw the way Ryan stared at me. It's like he wanted to apologize, yet; didn't want her to know about us either. Which brings me back to thinking he's ashamed of my weight.

I pulled up at my mother's house, got out and went to her room. She came home not too long ago and my father's been by her side. He still went to his house at night but made sure she was ok before leaving. You could still see the love they had for one another but in some cases, people live better apart. In which they do and it doesn't stop the love. In my opinion, I think my mom values him a lot more than she did previously.

"Hey ma." She walked out the bathroom.

"Hmph." No hello, or nothing; just attitude. Why do I even bother being round her?

"What?"

"He did something and now you're here sulking." I sat on her bed.

"He's messing with someone else."

"Well that's your fault. Who the hell sleeps with another man to piss the one she is in love with, off?" I turned to look at her.

"Don't roll your eyes at me. I may be a lotta things but stupid doesn't run through my blood."

"But.-"

"You don't have to convince me it wasn't what you did." I looked at her. Is it that obvious? Yes, I slept with Marcus to piss him off but I didn't plan on telling him unless he made me angry.

"What I wanna know is, if you claim he's ashamed and hurt you so bad, why be bothered? You like being fucked and dumped?" My mouth hit the floor.

160

"Obviously you do because that's what Mr. Banks is doing." Luna said coming in the room.

"How yo petty ass get in my house?" She held the key up. I gave her one in case something happened and I couldn't get there.

"Khloe, What the hell wrong with you giving my key to this hateful bitch?" She sat on the recliner chair in the corner, while Luna sat next to me.

"Hateful? Says the woman who's been a bitch and mean to her daughter since we were young."

"I'm gonna always be a bitch." She gave us a fake smile.

"And being mean and truthfully are two different things."

"How?" I wanted to know the difference.

"Being truthful requires a person to reveal things about someone they are already aware of and don't want to deal with it. Being mean, would require me to lie to you about shit and let you make a fool outta yourself." Was my mom serious?

"Explain!" I had my arms folded and so did Luna.

161

"All your life you've been fat." We both sucked our teeth.

"See what I mean. You want me to say plump, chunky or even thick when in reality you're fat. It is what it is." I rolled my eyes.

"Anyway, telling you the truth made you stronger. It made you demand respect from bitches and niggas off the street. You won't dare allow anyone to make you feel less of a woman. So, you're welcome." I sat there listening to her reasoning for treating me like shit. I understood but she went about it wrong.

"What about you only eating at expensive places and shopping on her dime?" Luna asked.

"Shit, if she got it, I'm gonna let her spend it on me."

"You're a loser." Luna was mad as hell she said that, where I didn't care. My mom was right. I let her get away with a lot and because of it, I was the one looking stupid. They say, a person will only do what you allow and that's my mom.

"Whatever. Call me what you want but tough love ain't never hurt nobody." She waved us off and walked down the steps.

"She's a hater. What's up with you? I tried to call but your phone is off."

"How'd you find me?"

"I knew you were here when I went to the house and your car was missing."

"Nothing. Ryan is sleeping with Raina's therapist."

"Ok so why you upset?" I snapped my neck to look at her.

"You basically told him to back off because you felt he was ashamed of you. Then your ass went and slept with the Marcus loser tryna hurt him. Which it did, I may add."

"What?"

"Yea, Waleed said he was mad as fuck you let another nigga touch you."

"Luna, he doesn't know what he wants."

"Ima keep it real with you Khloe." She stood in front of me.

"If you felt he was ashamed of you, why continue sleeping with him?" I looked at her because she wanted us together at one point.

"Yes, I was in your corner supporting because I'm your best friend and I'm supposed to. Just like if you said, let's go beat the therapist ass, I would." I laughed.

"I'm not fighting her."

"Anyway." She sucked her teeth. Luna loved to fight.

"Stop worrying about Ryan, if you don't want him. Stop getting upset when he's with someone else. Or do what's in your heart." She pointed to it.

"And what's that?"

"Go get your man."

"He doesn't want me anymore Luna."

"How do you know? Did you ask him?"

"No but the way she felt all over him told me it's a situation and I'm not sure I feel like being a side chick."

"Side chick? That nigga ain't making you a side chick. Waleed told me he was ready to show you off because that's how in love he was with you."

"Then why is he with her?"

"He needs some pussy. DUHHHHHHHH!" I started cracking up.

"He told you ever since you found him with that dumb bitch Veronica, he's been sleeping alone. Right?"

"Yea."

"Ok. That was a while ago. How long do you think he'd go without it?" I shrugged my shoulders.

"Get up."

"What?"

"Get yo ass up, go home, clean up and go get your man."

"I don't know where he is." She picked my phone up, asked me to unlock it and I saw her typing away.

"He's at his house packing." She showed me the text of her asking where he was.

"I don't know." She snatched my arm and started dragging me out the room. We got downstairs and my mom was on the couch with her head on my dad's lap.

"Is she?" Luna whispered and I almost threw up.

"Yooooo, she deep throating the hell out your dad. No wonder he ain't leave her." My dad's eyes were closed and he seemed to be enjoying it.

"Let's go." I led her out the back door so they didn't see us.

"Call me later boo." I told her.

"Shit after seeing that, I need to call Waleed and make him come over. I'm about to gobble his dick right up." I flicked her the finger and went to my car. I guess she's right about going to get Ryan. I am in love with him and if what she told me is true, he feels the same.

****

I parked in front of Ryan's spot and hated to go in. Raina hates this place and after the things she told me happened inside, I do too. Veronica did so many vile things to her, it's no wonder he made plans to move.

I knocked and the door opened. I guess he wasn't worried about no one coming over. I closed it behind me and noticed all the boxes throughout the living room. Some even had Lacey written on them. Raina told me once, that he kept

166

some of her things as a souvenir for her when she got older. He was definitely a great father to her.

"Ryan." I called out and walked around the downstairs looking for him. I made my way up the steps and heard his voice. It sounded like he was talking to someone. They had to be on the phone because no other car is here.

"You gotta go."

"You want me to go looking like this?" I heard a woman's voice and backed away from the door; only to knock a tote down the steps.

"What the fuck?" He shouted. I tried to get out fast but he caught me.

"Khloe?" I turned around and all he had on was a pair of black basketball shorts and a wife beater. Whoever the woman was had his dick hard, that's for sure.

"Ummm. Yea, sorry about just showing up. I thought you'd need help packing but I see you have company."

"Wait!" He took one step and she came out in a one-piece lingerie set. It was a bad piece but why is she coming out his room like that.

"Why is she here?" The fake ass girlfriend, therapist asked.

"I apologize Ryan. I didn't know you had company."

"It's fine Khloe. You ok?"

"I'm ok. Enjoy your night." I opened the door and speed walked to my car.

"Khloe." I stopped and wiped my eyes before turning around.

"What's wrong?" He used his thumb to wipe away the tears I missed.

"I messed up."

"What you mean?" He had his arms folded.

"I messed up with you. I tried to hurt you and, in the process, you found someone else." He smirked and it pissed me off.

"I'm in love with you Ryan and.-"

"And what?" I stopped when she came out the door still dressed in the one piece. I pointed and he turned around.

"Aye, are you fucking stupid? Take yo dumb ass back in the house and put some clothes on." She sucked her teeth but did it.

"I'm gonna go."

"You don't have to. She's leaving."

"I'm not going anywhere." This stalker was at the door. I had to grab his hand to keep him from running up and choking her. That's how angry he was.

"Ryan we'll talk tomorrow or the next day."

"No you won't. He's my man and it's shady as hell for you to show up unannounced." I let his hand go.

"Are you her man?" He ran his hand over his head.

"I'm so embarrassed."

"Embarrassed for what? You are always welcomed wherever Raina and I are?"

"I should've known you would never make someone like me your main chick. Why do I keep doing it to myself?" I looked over at the therapist who had an evil snarl on her face.

"Anytime we speak from now on, it will be strictly about Raina. I'm so sorry for intruding."

169

"Khloe, it's not what you think."

"Is it's not, then kiss me in front of her. Tell me how you feel out loud. Make it known that I'm who you want." He stared at me for a minute and stepped closer. I could feel his breath on my neck as he kissed it.

"I would do everything you asked if you wanted to be with me because of love and not to keep me away from her.

"Huh?"

"I'm in love with you too Khloe but after the stunt you pulled with dude, I'm not sure it's love or lust that you feel." I stood there looking stupid.

"She may not be the woman I want but until that woman finds me, she'll do. Good night K." He walked backwards to his house and slammed the door. There was nothing left to say. I guess he's done with me and all I can do is respect it.

Risky

I couldn't feel bad for Khloe because she finally admitted the reason she slept with dude, was to hurt me. It's fucked up that she had to go through childish measures to do it but I get it. I can say sorry a hundred times and she still won't be satisfied. Women are hard to understand but I was willing to show her that she's the only one I wanted. I made plans to take her away on vacation, then come back and show her off to everyone but it didn't work out that way. I guess it was a little too late in her eyes so she found comfort elsewhere.

Now this crazy bitch here, was starting to irk my nerves. I didn't know Khloe was coming over but I had an idea when the text came thru my phone, asking where I was. Unfortunately, Sandy popped up and since it was her first time here, asked for a tour.

I gave it to her and the last stop was the bedroom, in which I told her to get out and instead, she removed her clothes. Hell yea my dick got hard looking at her. However, I wouldn't sleep with her in this house because one... I was packing to move and unsure if Khloe would show up. And two... I didn't really feel like it. I had been ripping and running the streets so much looking for Veronica who I found, and this Oscar cat with Waleed. He was hiding well but it's a matter of time before he shows his face.

"What the hell is wrong with you?" I walked over to her on the couch.

"Ryan were supposed to be a couple, yet; you have females showing up to your house..." I stopped her.

"Did you hear yourself say my house?"

"What does that mean?"

"It means I can have who I want here. I already told you how close she is to Raina."

"I get it Ryan but Raina's not here and it's eleven at night. She didn't come here for your daughter. She came for you."

"Again. What goes on at my house is my business, not yours. As far as us being a couple, you were childish as hell for that lie."

"Fuck that Ryan. Love is written all over her face for you." I smirked.

"Not your business." I walked over to the door and opened it.

"You gotta go."

"What?"

"You heard me. You showed up here unannounced yourself but tryna check Khloe for doing the same. Then you brought yo ass outside the bedroom and house barely dressed, being funny. And before you lie and say it's not what you did. Save it." I ran up the steps and grabbed all her things. I handed them to her and pushed her out the door. Call me an asshole all you want but she doing too much.

"Ryan. Can we talk about this?"

"Not tonight." I slammed the door, locked it and took my ass to sleep on the couch. Both women were driving me crazy.

****

"It's pretty packed in here tonight." Waleed said and sat down. We were at the club hoping to see Oscar or even Julie,

173

who's been calling him and asking for another chance. Mighty funny how she wanted him now that he's with her sister.

"Yea it is. How long we staying?" I'm usually ok staying out half the night but I promised to take Raina to the mall tomorrow and she takes forever. You would swear she was a grownup.

After Khloe and Luna beat those kids up at the school, Raina has become super popular and wanted to make sure she looked nice. I had to instill in her not to change who she was, because if they didn't like her before, they still don't. Kids tend to flock to whoever is hot and right now my daughter is. It'll die down soon and hopefully, we won't have any issues. I hope not anyway.

"Ima fuck Luna up." He put his beer down and walked down the steps. Here she was six months and in the club. Not only that, we were expecting Oscar and since he's mad Waleed said they weren't getting married, it's no telling what he'll do if he sees her. We're not even sure how he found out because neither of us have caught up to him.

I went behind him and grinned when I noticed Khloe next to her. As usual her outfit was nice and they fit perfect.

"What the fuck you doing here?" Waleed started snapping.

"Can I get a lemon drop shot and a Margarita?" Khloe asked the bartender and she disappeared to get it for her. I pulled money out and placed it on the counter.

"It's ok Ryan. I got it." She smiled and pushed the money towards me.

"You don't ever have to pay for anything in my presence K."

"Here you go." The lady took the money and moved on to the next customer.

"Let's go Luna." Waleed snatched her up and took her outside. I took a seat next to Khloe and noticed some lipstick on the side and wiped it.

"You sure it's ok to touch me? I would hate for your pit bull girlfriend to show up."

"She's not my girlfriend."

"Does she know that?" Both of us laughed.

She and I sat there enjoying each other's company. A few chicks came over tryna get my attention but Khloe was the only one who had it. Waleed ended up taking Luna home, so K had to get a ride with me.

"Aye. That's enough." I pushed the drink away from her and made her stand. She was wobbly and definitely tipsy if not drunk. I didn't even pay it any mind on how much she was drinking because I knew she wasn't going home with anyone.

"Let's go." I took her hand in mine and headed to the door and stopped.

"Oooooh. You're in trouble." She busted out laughing.

"Ryan, she looks mad." She kept laughing at Sandy's facial expression. I didn't make it better by laughing with her.

"What's this?" Sandy pointed to my hand holding Khloe's.

"She needs a ride home. I'll be back."

"I'm coming with you."

"Bitch, he don't need a supervisor. Plus, I may wanna get nasty and you're not invited to watch." K used her index finger to mush her in the forehead. Sandy and her friend started talking shit.

"Yo. Take yo ass in the bar. I'll be back in a half hour."

"You better or I'm coming to find you."

"Ughhhh stalker." Sandy went to swing on Khloe and I cut that shit short.

"You on some other shit yo."

"Why? Because I don't want my man taking another bitch home?"

"One... I ain't your man and two... you tryna swing off knowing she's intoxicated. Fuck outta here."

"Oh she's drunk alright." I turned and Khloe was all in some guys face and he wasn't moving her away. He was about to put his hands on her ass.

CLICK! My gun was on his forehead.

"You can have any chick in there bro, but this one is off limits." He put his hands up and backed away. I didn't bother turning around to see Sandy.

"Get in."

"Ryan you have someone. Why are you stopping me from being with a guy?" I ignored her and listened to her rant and cry about loving me, and me loving another woman. I knew a drunk person speaks a sober thought. I also know she was tore up and would probably apologize tomorrow.

I parked in front of her house, took the keys out her hand and opened the door. She almost fell when she got out but I held onto her. Once we got inside, I locked the door and helped her up the steps. For her it seemed like forever and me, I wanted her to lie down and feel better. Unfortunately, after we stepped in the room she kicked her shoes off, removed her shirt and jeans and hopped in the bed. My mind told me to leave but my heart and dick forced me to stay.

"Lock up when you leave please." She pulled the covers over her and I removed them.

"Why are you?-" She stopped and looked.

"You're gonna get in a lotta trouble tryna stay the night." She pulled the covers up and lifted them up for me to join.

"I'm where I wanna be." I took the covers back off again, grabbed both of her ankles, pulled her to the edge of the bed and spread her legs.

"Ryan this isn't... Oh my Gawdddddd." She grabbed the sheets and arched her back as a strong orgasm came rushing out. Her pearl was thumping, which let me know she wasn't finished and needed more.

"You still love me Khloe?" I rubbed the tip over her clit and enjoyed seeing her body shake.

"I can't hear you."

"AHHHHHHH." She dug her nails in my arms when I forcefully entered her hidden treasure.

"Yes baby. Yes. I'm still in love with you." She pulled me down and our tongues danced together. Her bottom half was grinding on mine as I penetrated her harder, faster and deeper. I hit her so deep, her eyes rolled and her voice was no longer there.

"Now whose pussy is this?"

"Yours baby. It always will be. Fuck! I'm cumming again. Ryannnnnnnn!" I watched her essence seep out and onto my dick.

"I wanna get on top." She slurred and at first, I refused but she kept whining.

"Got damn, you're gonna make me cum fast." She placed both of her hands in mine, leaned in for a kiss and rode the fuck outta me. I don't think a woman has ever done me this good. Not that I can remember, anyway.

"You love me Ryan." I released her hands from mine and grabbed her face with both hands to make her look at me.

"I'm in love with you K. Let me put a baby in you to prove I want us and a family with you." I felt something wet and saw the tears falling down her face.

"Stop crying." She wiped her face and I kept her grinding on top.

"You're mine baby and I swear I'm yours." My body started stiffening up.

"Yea K. I'm about to drop my son in you and I swear if you take a plan b, I'm gonna fucking kill you." She looked shocked.

"Ryan." I know she was wondering how I knew. Shit, it's the only thing I could think of since she never came to tell me she was pregnant. What else could it be?

"It's in the past. Don't do it again and we good." She nodded and squeezed those inside muscles together and a nigga held her there until every baby swam into her body. Oh she's definitely gonna be pregnant by morning.

Khloe

Bzzz. Bzzzzzz. Bzzzzz.

"Ughhhhh." I tossed the cover off my head to answer my phone that wouldn't stop ringing. I picked it up and put my arm over my eyes because the sun was bright as hell.

"Hello!" I snapped.

"Where's Ryan?" I looked at the phone and realized it wasn't mine. I looked on the side of me and he was right there, knocked out on his stomach.

"Hold on." I nudged him and he stirred a little.

"Ryan."

"Yea."

"I answered your phone by accident. Here?" I thought he would've been upset or even snap. All he did was turn over, smile and take it from me.

"Yo. Who this?" I rolled back on my side and threw the covers over me. My head was pounding and just the little bit of movement down below, had an aching feeling.

"What you want man?" He turned and pulled me closer. I felt his dick at my ass and decided to fuck with him.

"Don't worry about what I do with my woman."

"Your woman? Since when?" I heard the chick say. I moved under the covers and tapped his leg so he could lie on his back.

"That's all me on you?" There was cum covering his entire dick. He grinned and nodded yes.

"Well let me take it off." I opened my mouth, relaxed my throat and gave him one hell of a blow job.

"Awwwww fuck K." He gripped the sheet with one hand.

"Yo! I gotta go. Got damnnnn K." I heard the phone hit the floor. My hands were on his side as I went up and down without them.

"Shit. Make me cum for you Khloe." I gave him exactly what he wanted. It was too early to have sperm in my mouth but for him, I didn't mind.

After he came, I kissed and sucked up his entire body. Hickeys were in some places and I laughed because I left them there on purpose. I could feel him growing and placed his semi hard dick inside. He bit down on his lip and fucked the hell outta me from the bottom. I ended up tapping out on top and let him have his way with me.

"You pregnant K." He grabbed my hand and led me in the bathroom.

"Who said that?" He reached in and turned the shower on.

"I'm claiming it and you better not go to any stores. I'm not playing."

"I won't. Did you mean what you said about being all mine?" I was a mess last night but heard him say that.

"Nah. I only said it to get you to fuck the shit outta me." My mouth fell open.

"I'm just kidding. I meant every word K." He kissed me and got on his knees. I knew he wasn't proposing so it was expected to feel him feasting on my goodies. I loved giving Ryan head and evidently; he felt the same towards me.

"Now turn over and let me get some before I take Raina shopping." He never gave me the chance to respond. His ass literally had me moaning and tryna scratch the walls from how good it felt.

****

"I'll be back later." He kissed my lips and told me to lock up behind him. I went back upstairs, took the sheets and blankets off to wash and started cleaning my house. It was Saturday and what I did normally anyway.

I had the music blasting and was in my zone when I heard the doorbell ring. Not too many people knew where I lived and those who did, had a key. Well, except Ryan but he usually calls before he comes. I opened it and sucked my teeth. This is the second time one of his flunky's showed up after finding out about us. I turned the music down from my remote and stood there staring at this gorgeous woman. I'm not gonna hate. Sandy is beautiful, smart and had a body to match. However, I'm not about to be intimidated by her either.

"How can I help you?"

"Well first off, you can tell me why you played drunk and seduced my man." She had the nerve to say and I snickered.

185

"Honey, I don't need to play drunk in order for him to sleep with me. What the fuck is wrong with you and your man?" I was now standing face to face with her.

"Yes, my man." I noticed two other chicks getting out the car and heading towards us. I see now, she wanted a fight. I couldn't contact Luna because she was pregnant and Waleed would kill me if she lost the baby so it was about to be a three on one but best believe, I'm knocking at least one out.

"Well how is he your man, when he stayed here all night and just left not too long ago? I know you heard him when he asked, why are you questioning him about his woman, which is me?" I pointed to myself and noticed her friends looking around.

"If you're sucking his dick, of course he'd call you that." I thought about what she said and laughed. I was definitely giving him head when he said it but not when he told me in the shower. That was all him.

"What do you want Sandy?"

"For you to leave him alone. We were doing fine those weeks you weren't speaking to him."

"Sandy, you should have a sit down with yourself because you clearly have issues."

"Bitch!" She swung and I ducked.

"Oh yea." I punched her in the nose and kept on hitting. I also felt other hits, which meant they were jumping me.

"What the hell?" I heard some guys voice and felt him pull me off her.

"Go inside Khloe." I looked at the guy and it was one of Risky's friends. I didn't really know who he was but I've seen him around.

"Hell no. I want these bitches outta here." I ran up on Sandy and started beating her ass some more.

"Oh hell no." I could hear Luna cursing in Spanish. I looked over after the guy pulled me of Sandy again and Waleed was holding her.

"I got something for you Khloe." Sandy screamed out, wiping blood off her mouth.

"Get yo stupid ass outta here."

"Waleed, I know you not acting funny when you just had your dick all up in this pussy two weeks ago." It was like everyone stopped; including Luna. Whoever the chick was that came with Sandy claimed to have been sleeping with him.

"Yea, you fucking this fat bitch, yet; begging to dig deep in these walls." Luna had no facial expression. Waleed walked up on the chick, pulled his gun out and shot her in the face.

"OH MY GOD!" All of us yelled at the same time. I knew he was crazy but this is beyond that.

"Which one of you bitches is next?" Both of them stood there in shock, right along with me.

"Sandy, you know Risky don't even rock with you on any level, other than fucking. Why you over here? And you..." He put his gun on the girls' forehead and she instantly started crying.

"Your sister knows the type of nigga I am so she asked for this. I suggest you and your stuck-up ass friend keep your mouth shut or I promise you're both next."

"Did you have to kill her?" The chick asked.

"I'll kill anyone for tryna make my wife leave me, especially when the shit ain't true. Fuck you think this is?" I snapped my neck to look at Luna because they're not married as far as I know. This bitch had the audacity to smirk and shrug her shoulders.

"Bitch, you better hope Risky don't make you suffer the same fate. Now get your stupid ass outta here." Sandy ran but the sister begged Waleed to let her take the body. After cursing her out and saying she'd be at the funeral home, she finally left.

Waleed had some guys clean up the mess and him and the guys walked to the few neighbor's house I had, to see if either of them were home. I lived in a cult de sack so it was only six houses. Luckily, none of them were home because I'd hate to see what he would do.

Luna

"Say what?" I heard Waleed shout. We were on our way back from my parents' house when someone called and told him something but I didn't know what. We stayed the night there because Waleed was so damn drunk I couldn't get his ass up.

"Aight. I'm on my way." He hung up and looked at me.

"When we get here, you better not get in it."

"In what?" He ignored me and continued driving. Once we pulled up at Khloe's and saw those bitches, I tried to get over there but he caught me. Two dudes were breaking the fight up and by the time it was all said and done, a bitch died and two others ran away with their tail stuck between their legs.

"Stay here until I come back." Waleed smacked me on the ass and shut the door. Khloe stood there with her arms folded staring at me.

"What?"

"Bitch, don't what me. What the fuck is this?" She lifted my left hand that held my wedding ring on it.

"Oh we got married last night."

"WHATTTTTT?"

"Its a long story."

"It's a long story my ass. You didn't even call. What the fuck?" I could tell how upset she was. I didn't know if her anger stemmed from those chicks showing up or that she's really mad I got married without her being there.

"Khloe, it was last minute."

"Fuck that last-minute shit Luna. I'm your best friend, your sister. How could you not tell me? I would've never done you like that."

"Khloe, are you seriously this mad over.-" I couldn't finish.

"Hell fucking yea. Would you be ok with me having a secret/ last minute wedding? Then I come over all non chalant on some oh well shit." I understood because I'd be going off.

"Khloe."

"You know what Luna. Just go."

"What?"

"Go. I got a lot going on and then you hit me this and give me, a you'll get over it attitude." The door opened and in walked Waleed, Raina and Risky.

"You good?" Risky started checking her over.

"I'm fine."

"What's wrong?" He asked her.

"I'm just over the bullshit. I finally got what I wanted from you and that's to be your one and only. Then this dumb chick comes over telling me to leave you alone because you're her man. She fights me and makes idle threats as she leaves to scare me. And let's not forget my fucking best friend jumped the broom last night and ain't told a soul."

"Khloe." Waleed tried to say something.

"Don't Waleed. Last minute or not, she should've told me."

"I thought you knew. I was gonna bring you but since you never mentioned it I thought you didn't want to." Risky told her but you could tell she was confused.

"Huh?"

"Yea. That's why they left the club last night." Him saying that only made it worse.

"HOLD THE FUCK UP!" Khloe was standing in my face and Waleed pulled me back.

"You said it was last minute but you knew at the bar?"

"I was gonna tell you but Risky sat next to you and I noticed how happy you were. I didn't wanna interrupt your happiness."

"GET THE FUCK OUT!" She pointed to the door.

"Aunt Luna you married my uncle?" Raina questioning me had me feeling worse. She's always said if we got married she wanted to be a bridesmaid.

"Waleed, take your wife out my house. I don't deal with sheisty ass bitches."

"Khloe, you need to calm down." I was now in her face. This time Waleed started pushing me out the door.

"Luna you know it ain't shit to get it poppin." Were we really about to fight over me not telling her?

"Whoaaaa." Risky said and pushed her back.

"Right after I drop my son. We sure can."

"Well damn. I guess that slipped your mind. Right?" I forgot to tell her we were having a boy too.

"Aunt Luna, I thought Khloe was like your sister." I wanted to smack Raina for butting in.

"RAINA!" Her father shouted.

"No dad. If I were Ms. K, I'd be mad too. They do everything together. Why wouldn't she tell her about the wedding or baby? That's not right." She stormed up the steps and you heard the door slam.

"I'm sorry Khloe. I wasn't thinking and..."

"This is my last time telling you to get the fuck out my house." Risky was still standing in front of her and Waleed was pulling me out the door.

"It's like that?"

"It's how you made it." She rolled her eyes and walked towards the kitchen.

"Risky can you.-"

"Nope."

"You didn't even let me ask."

"I'm not getting in the middle of y'all shit." He closed the door behind us and walked down the steps.

"Luna, I had no idea you didn't tell her. Now I'm gonna have to figure out how to make shit good."

"How you figure?"

"Duh. We just made it official last night and now she knows I knew about y'all shotgun wedding and she didn't."

"Whatever."

"That's your problem right there." I turned around and stared at him. Waleed was talking to the other dudes who were there prior to us arriving.

"You have an I don't care attitude about shit because it's not affecting you."

"What you mean?"

"I'm saying, how you forget to tell her the two most important things in your life? If that were her you would be cursing her out. Then you act like it's not that serious because like I said, it's not affecting you."

"I thought she would wanna be with you..."

"Save it. Regardless if she did or not, there's no way she would've missed it. You know as well as I, that Khloe would have stopped whatever she was doing to be there. But if that's what you need to tell yourself in order to sleep at night, have at it."

"I honestly didn't look at it like that."

"You and Khloe have been friends for years. Y'all did everything together and I'm sure have gone through a lot of hard times as well. For you to overlook all of it and say, you didn't look at it like that makes me wonder if you were really her friend."

"WHAT?"

"A real friend should never forget to invite her bestie. You see Waleed told me." He shrugged and left me standing in my thoughts. The way he described it, made it seem a lot worse. But in all honesty, I really thought she'd wanna be with him.

"Get yo ass in the car." Waleed shouted and opened the door for me.

"What? You mad too?"

"Hell yea. How you tryna fight your best friend over some shit you did? Girl you testing the hell outta me. Lose my son if you want." He slammed the door and almost hit me. I stuck my finger up.

"You will later."

****

"I was wondering why she wasn't here and I agree with Khloe." My mom said and passed me some grapes to eat.

"So everyone hates Luna now."

"Girl stop talking in third person." She wiped her hands on the apron wrapped around her waist. She was making dinner for all of us and invited Khloe, who of course declined.

"You can look at it however you want but the fact remains that you were dead wrong. Now I have your back on just about everything but I can't on this." She lifted my face with her index finger.

"Not only did you disregard your best friends' feelings, you left her out of one of the most important things in your life. Then, you failed to mention my grandson and you knew about him a week ago. What's going on with you?" I put my head down and started crying.

"This baby has me all over the place. One minute I'm happy. The next, I'm sad then I forgot to tell my best friend two important things and she won't talk to me. Oscar's gonna kill me for marrying someone else and getting pregnant. And there's no telling where that demon child is lurking."

"Honey the only thing you should concern yourself with right now is my grandbaby."

"What about Khloe?"

"I love Khloe like my own daughter and what you did is foul but the baby in your stomach doesn't need to go through the motions. If you want one less thing to stress about, call her up and apologize."

"Ma, I tried…" She put her hand up and cut me off.

"No, you gave her some, *bullshit ass, oh well, I'm sorry apology.*" My mom rolled her eyes.

"Luna, me and your father spoiled you all your life and I know you feel like apologizing is beneath you and Khloe knows it too. But you're gonna have to do it. And if it's not sincere, I don't see Khloe ever speaking to you again."

"She wouldn't stop speaking to me forever, for something like this." My mom raised her eyebrow.

"Don't underestimate what a person would do when they're hurt." She patted me on the back and left me in the kitchen with my own thoughts.

I picked my phone up and sent Khloe a message but put it back down when Waleed text and told me to bring my ass home. He is gonna be the death of me. Let me not say that because he may be, if Oscar finds out about my situation before Waleed kills him. I picked my things up and went to the front door where my dad was just coming in. I kissed him on the cheek and drove home.

Waleed

"What the fuck is she so mad about?" Luna asked when she came in the house. After the fiasco over Khloe's, she had the nerve to take her anger out on me. I dropped her ass right off to my mother in law. Damn, it sounds crazy as fuck to say but it's true. She and I did get married quick. To be honest, I would've asked her to marry me eventually, but after her pops contacted and gave me an offer I couldn't refuse, I had no problem walking down the aisle and tying the knot. And yes Luna is aware of everything her dad and I spoke about.

The day he called, I was about to see Oscar, who I found out never left town. Evidently, he started fucking some chick here in the states and no one knew who it was. Never mind, he had been over here tryna recruit niggas on a team he'd never have and guess who's on the top of his list? Yup, Lamar which doesn't surprise me at all. Hearing that made me change my entire set up. I purchased new properties for the traps and changed delivery, pickup and drop off times. Lamar, isn't a nigga I'd ever trust. Plus, him and dirty ass Dora already broke in one before. I know he wouldn't have a problem doing it again.

Anyway, her pops met me at Risky's funeral parlor. No one would think he'd be making business plans there so in our eyes it was a perfect place to meet. Risky had his employees stay home on a paid day off while we discussed the future with Luna's pop.

He told me about the agreement between him and the Oscar's guy father. It stated that she had to marry Oscar by the age of twenty-five, in order to run her father's empire. Or should I say, it's what it was supposed to say. The day Luna went home accusing him of knowing about a different agreement made him look at the original one. He still had it in an envelope that had never been opened since the birth of Oscar, who is the same age as Luna.

Long story short, everything was in there as far as, her needing to be married by the age of twenty-five and her father had to agree to it. As luck would have it, whoever the lawyer was left out the groom being Oscar and put he could be anyone

Luna's father chose instead. The crazy part is, Oscars father must not gave noticed because he signed it too.

After talking to him we met again at his house the next day with a different lawyer. The one who drew up their final papers passed away a few years ago. The new one said, the document is legal and even if they tried to contest it, a judge wouldn't go against it. Once that was clear, he asked if I would marry his daughter. His only stipulation was to be involved silently with the business. I told him he could run it for all I care and that Luna wasn't marrying Oscar regardless. I'm not a greedy nigga so I could care less.

Yesterday he told us, his friend, who is the mayor would come by to marry us. Being Luna and I discussed it the previous night, we agreed to get it done so when Oscar found out it wouldn't be nothing he could do. She was supposed to wait for me at her mom's while I tried to see if Oscar would show up, since I put word on the street, that if anyone saw him, this is where I'd be. But her non-listening ass came to the club with Khloe.

Of course, I'm pissed because Oscar sneaky as fuck and a shoot-out could happen at any time. I'll be damned if anyone shot her. I snatched her up and saw Risky speaking to Khloe. We left and once we got to the house, I text to see if he were coming but he said Khloe was so drunk he had to drive her home.

I understood and he was still gonna be the best man in the big wedding Luna has planned. This was some quick shit and the only ones there were me, Luna, her parents and the damn Mayor. I never even thought to ask her questions about Khloe. I thought maybe she was getting drunk before the wedding and couldn't hang. A nigga had no idea she didn't know, so I feel her pain. Luna's her best friend and never mentioned that or my son. Yet, she sitting here wondering why Khloe mad. Is she serious?

"Oh she not supposed to be?" I opened the box of food she picked up for me at the soul food place.

"She's still gonna be in the big wedding. I don't..." I put my hand up and bit into the BBQ ribs. I didn't wanna hear shit as I savored the taste.

"Ok you think because it's gonna be another wedding, she should be fine?" I put a forkful of baked macaroni and cheese in my mouth.

"Well yea."

"I hate to tell you this but it didn't work like that." I took a few more bites and moved over to her.

"Khloe, ain't one of your servants ma."

"I know that."

"Do you?" I could see an attitude forming but she knows that shit don't bother me.

"You can't leave her out thinking it's ok because she's been around for a while. How would you feel if her and my boy got married and she didn't tell you? Then found out the sex of their baby and knowing you're the godmother, she never said a word." She sat there looking crazy.

"You can get mad at me all you want but you foul as fuck for that."

"Wale."

"Don't call me that?"

"Why not? Everyone else does."

204

"Everyone is not my wife."

"But my sister did." I cringed listening to her bring Julie up. Not only are they sisters but I was in serious relationships with both of them.

"I asked her not to call me Wale and she did it anyway."

"What's the difference?"

"The difference is she was my girl at the time and Wale is a street name. I don't want my woman referring to me the same as, the niggas off the street. Now that you're my wife, you definitely don't need to call me Wale."

"Fine! I'll call you Leed then."

"Or daddy." I smiled and she smacked me on the side of my arm.

"How do I make it up to her?"

"To be honest, I can't even tell you."

"What about asking Risky to.-"

"I'm not asking him shit. You can. And how you tryna get him to fix what you broke?"

"Ok well then don't expect no cum facials and..."

"The fucking lies you tell." I grabbed her hand and slid it in my jeans.

"You're not holding out on anything regarding sex because you fucked up. Matter of fact, my dick hard and since I was forced to marry you, I think…"

"Forced?"

"Yea because if I didn't marry your chunky ass, I would've had to kill any man your pops tried to get you with."

"Oh yea." She removed her hand, unbuttoned my jeans and slid them and my boxers down.

"Yea."

"Well, if my husband wants his wife to satisfy his needs, he has to help me and my friend speak again."

"Not a chance." She got up off the chair, kneeled down and did some things that had a nigga damn near screaming out.

"You like the way I suck your dick, Leed?" When she said that it turned me on even more. My nut was dying to release.

"What the hell you doing?" She looked up with a grin on his face.

"I gave you head but it wasn't to make you cum." My dick was hurting and she was playing.

"Aight Luna. Damn. Finish me off." I stroked myself but it felt nowhere near as good as when she did it.

"Promise."

"Yea baby. Come on please." I was begging to get her to let me release.

"You better not be lying." She had her arms folded. The longer she took, the angrier I became.

"I'm telling you if I have to make myself nut, I'm not doing shit." She moved over to me.

"You better not get up." I grabbed her hair and came extremely hard. A nigga had to sit because my knees were weak.

"If you ever do that again, I'm gonna..." I was breathing hard as hell.

"You ain't doing shit. Now come upstairs and fuck me." Why my dick twitch when she said that.

However, once I got it together, guess who had her legs touching her ears and screaming. I had no mercy on her;

especially after she tried to play me. I bet her ass won't do it again.

Khloe

"So you and the Mexican not speaking huh?" My mom asked as I was on the last batch of fried chicken, I was making for dinner. This is the first time she's been to my house since she left the hospital. Its taken her a while to get it together but as you can tell her mouth ain't change.

I came back to my house because Ryan told me his ex is no longer among the living. I never questioned his actions because one... he just became my man and two... whatever punishment he handed down to her, she deserved it for all the pain and suffering she put his daughter through.

"Mrs. Banks, calling Luna Mexican is racist." Raina told her.

"Who was talking to you little girl?"

"Did anyone ever tell you, you're rude, ignorant, and a pain in the a..."

"RAINA!" I stopped her before she could finish. Her and my mother would go at it.

"Ms. K, she does not have to talk about Luna. Especially, when she's nowhere around to defend herself."

"I ain't scared of that bitch."

"Oh now she a bitch. Maybe I should call her over here to whoop your..." I had to laugh a little because Raina seemed to be more stronger and opinionated than ever before. Her self-confidence was at an all-time high now and she claimed, to not have any more issues with bullies.

The thing I loved the most about Raina is, she didn't let what Veronica or Bridget do, stop her from living her life. I mean she did at first but once she told everyone, its like a weight was lifted and she felt better. I guess she knew her father would handle it and even though he did it ass backwards, he did it.

"RAINA! Upstairs." I pointed and she pouted, grabbed her things and stormed up the steps. I wasn't tryna be her mother but she was definitely going to respect adults. Even the ones she may not like. Well let me rephrase that. Adults who aren't violating her in any way, shape or form.

"You're gonna let her speak to me like that?" My mother poured another glass of wine as I rubbed my temples, trying to decide if I wanna kick her out.

"Ma, did you forget that she's a child?"

"Child my ass."

"Whether she's mature for her age or not, Raina is only twelve. Regardless of Luna and I speaking or not, you can't say what you want to, or in front of her."

"Maybe that's the problem." I looked up.

"Tell me what the problem is since you know so much." I picked the fork up and removed the chicken from the oil and place it on the plate covered with paper towels. I hated greasy chicken. I shut the stove off and started straightening up a little before making the plates. I was tired and hopefully my mom would get the hint and leave, but I could never get so lucky.

"First off, she has no respect for adults. Second... the little heffa don't know her place and should never involve herself in grown folks conversations." She was getting on my nerves.

"Just because those kids bullied her and that crazy woman moles..." I slammed the rag down and moved in her face.

"Don't you ever bring that shit up." I yelled shocking myself. I have never talked back to my mother.

"Excuse me."

"You heard what the fuck I said." She put her wine glass down and stood up.

"Say whatever you want to or about me, I don't care. I've dealt with it all my life so it no longer bothers me but what you won't do is terrorize, intimidate, humiliate, embarrass or make that child feel like it's her fault for having a guard up because of what she's been through."

"Khloe."

"No ma. You think she wanted any of that to happen to her? You think she liked being bullied at school or probably needing therapy all her life due to some sick person? What the fuck is wrong with you?"

"Let go K." I heard and didn't realize my hands were wrapped around my mother's throat until Ryan pried them off.

"Oh my God. Ma, I didn't mean to." I backed away, threw my apron I was wearing on the floor, grabbed my keys and ran out the house.

"KHLOE! KHLOE!" I heard Ryan yelling but I closed my car door and sped out my driveway. What was I thinking putting my hands on my mother? My dad is going to kill me.

I stopped at the light and went to pick my phone up to call my dad but it wasn't in here. I realized in a rush to leave, I left it. Maybe it's what's best at the moment. I didn't wanna snap on anyone and the only person who could understand me is Luna and I'm not fucking with her right now. Call me petty or whatever but she was dead ass wrong for not telling me.

I went in my dad's house and he was on the phone. I put my fingers to my lips, asking him not to reveal where I am. He finished the conversation with whom I'm assuming is my mother, hung up and stared at me. He didn't say anything at first and I think it was to give me a moment to collect myself.

"It's about time baby." He said and hugged me tight. I broke down and sobbed like a kid.

213

"I'm sorry daddy. She was talking about the things Raina went through and I snapped." He rubbed my back. I looked up at him.

"She's been through enough and I may be able to handle her ignorance but I would never put Raina through the torture."

"Let me tell you something about your mother that I've never said to anyone." I wiped my eyes with the back of my hand.

"Your mother was and still is the love of my life." I sucked my teeth.

"There's nothing I wouldn't do for that woman and she knew it, which is why we were in debt. Needless to say, when she became pregnant with you, the only thing on her mind was having a daughter." I rolled my eyes.

"I'm serious. It was always, I can't wait to dress her up, show her off and all the different things she wanted to do with you." He moved my hair out my face.

"We never found out the sex of the baby so when it was time to deliver, neither of us could wait." I noticed sadness on his face.

"What happened?"

"Your mom had to have a C-section due to you being a breech baby. Khloe, after you came out, it was love at first sight for us." I smiled because at least she loved me at some point.

"Unfortunately, as the doctor cleaned her out he noticed an extensive amount of bleeding and they had to do an emergency surgery." I covered my mouth.

"Evidently, one of her Fallopian tubes burst and she got a nasty infection. It was so bad, they had to give her a hysterectomy."

"I'm so sorry dad."

"I never thought about it until I moved out but I think she blames you for not being able to bear more of my kids."

"It's not my fault."

"She knows that but your mom wanted a big family and once they told her it could only happen through adoption, she went into a deep depression. I had to take a leave of absence at work because she refused to take care of you."

"Did she ever get it together?"

"She did when you were two months old. She still dressed you up, took you out and showed you off. However, the older and prettier you became, the more her hatred grew and don't ask me why because I have no idea how she could be jealous of her own flesh and blood."

"I thought you says she hates me because she couldn't have kids." Now I was confused.

"Your mom got over that. The reason she became jealous is because out of all her mother's kids, you were the only granddaughter. Your two uncles both had boys. Therefore; they spoiled you rotten and the attention her brothers used to give her, went to you." I had to chuckle because my uncles and male cousins still to this day, will drop whatever they're doing to help me. Both of my uncles ripped my mom a new asshole anytime it was a family gathering and she said something disrespectful. I mean embarrassed the shit outta her and didn't care.

216

"That's not my fault either."

"No it's not Khloe. But the way they protected and shielded you from everything and everyone made her bitter. They weren't supposed to love you more than her."

"Why didn't you ever tell me?"

"I never paid it any mind because I was working a lot and tryna deal with her attitude. Now that I'm alone all the time, I've been thinking about things and it's the only reason I could come up with." I nodded and laid my head on his shoulder. At least, I had a better idea of why she was mean to me. And I'm not falling for that difference between mean and truthful shit she tried to run on me.

"I'm sorry for not paying better attention and allowing her to treat you like shit." He kissed my forehead.

"It's ok dad." He lifted my head.

"Khloe, I know this has nothing to do with anything but Ryan is a good man and he is in love with you."

"Ummmm. I'm not sure why you brought him up."

"Because as you were coming in, I heard him in the background telling your mother to leave and if she ever hurts you again in any way, she's gonna regret it."

"What?"

"Don't you dare get upset."

"I'm not. I just didn't expect him to say anything to her."

"Whatever spell you have on him, he won't allow anyone to disrespect you."

"I'm scared dad. What if I'm not good enough for him? What if he sees a better-looking woman and sleeps with her? What if..."

"Don't speak it into existence. Continue to love him and his daughter and I don't ever see you two separating."

"Thanks dad. Do you mind if I stay here tonight?"

"Unless, we're sleeping together in this house, you'll be in my bed." I turned around and Ryan was standing there smiling.

"How did you know where I was?" I stood up and he walked over.

"I will always know where my woman is." He placed a soft and gentle kiss on my lips.

"Are you ok?" I could see the concern on his face.

"Yea. I don't know what came over me. She was talking slick and I snapped."

"You don't have to explain anything to me. We all know that was a long time coming." He took my hand in his.

"Come on, I have a surprise for you."

"A surprise?"

"Yes, now hurry up."

"Wait! Where's Raina? I know you didn't leave her."

"I dropped her off to my mom's. Mr. Banks, I hate to be rude but we got plans."

"We do."

"Yup. And don't worry about the food you were cooking. Everything is off and your door is locked." I kissed my father goodbye and promised to call in the morning. I couldn't wait to see what my surprise was.

Risky

When I walked in, I heard Mrs. Banks talking shit about my daughter and by the time I reached the kitchen, it was already too late because Khloe was ready to kill her. I had to control my laugh as I stood there watching my girl, choke her mother. Khloe, must've been squeezing the life outta her because Mrs. Banks eyes were damn near popping out her head. I didn't expect Khloe to run off but wasn't surprised either. That's probably the first time she's ever talked back to her mom or laid hands on her. And to know it's over Raina, only confirmed she's the woman I need in my life.

She adores my daughter and isn't afraid to discipline her. Not that I allow anyone to do it besides me, my mom and Waleed but Khloe has motherly instincts. I also know she's teaching her how to be a woman and respect herself. Something I'm not sure Veronica ever took the time to do. It's all good tho because that's one less person off this earth who won't bother another child.

"Where are we going?" Khloe asked when I entered the turnpike.

"Dinner."

"Dinner? You better not be taking me a rest stop to eat." I busted out laughing and swerved a little.

"Just relax K." I took her hand in mine and kissed the back of it. This woman had me deep in love and she didn't even know it. And before anyone talks shit, I am fully aware of how much I fucked up with her. Ima win my woman back whether y'all like it or not. Thank you readers for all the hate, but I got this."

"We're here." I pulled up in front of the Ritz Carlton and valet opened the door for both of us.

"Ryan, I'm not dressed for this." I walked around to her side and held her hand.

"You look gorgeous." She had on a pair of black leggings, a blue shirt and some black air max's. I pecked her lips and we stepped inside.

"Ummmm. Ryan, this place is for rich people." Her head was spinning as she took in the hotel.

"People are staring at us." I laughed because no one paid us any mind. I guess when you feel uncomfortable it seems like it.

"Hello, Mr. Wells. Is this the woman?" The hotel manager asked with a smile on his face. Khloe had a shocked look on hers. I had been back and forth all week to make sure tonight was perfect.

"Yup. This is her."

"Beautiful, just like you said." He kissed her hand and Khloe had the nerve to blush.

"Mary, it's time." He said and a woman came over and asked Khloe to follow her. I went up to the extra room to change clothes. It was on the top floor and close to the roof.

I put the black Tom Ford suit on after showering and had to admire myself in the mirror. I'm not conceited by any means but I do take pride in my appearance. I picked my things up, the extra key and walked down the hall to take the elevator upstairs. I purchased three rooms this evening, one for me, one for Khloe to change in and the last one is where her biggest surprise is at.

After I checked in the other room to make sure it was set up correctly, I went to the end of the hall and stepped out on the roof. The table had a red and black table cloth on it, along with long and short candles to match. There were two place settings and a dozen roses in her seat. I love you balloons were tied to the chairs and a chef stood there waiting to be told what to make. I had no idea what she wanted so he's here to make whatever. I looked to my left and the band I hired were starting to play music.

"Mr. Wells." I turned around when the manager called me.

"Your date is here." I nodded and once he opened the door, a nigga not only lost his breath but had to grab myself by how gorgeous she was.

Khloe wore a long red dress with two splits on the side. The red bottoms on her feet looked uncomfortable but she didn't say a word. Her hair flowed down her back and the makeup was barely there, which I appreciated. She didn't need all that on her face. The diamond necklace, matching earrings and tennis bracelet accentuated the outfit perfect. The crazy part is, Luna came shopping with me and picked the entire outfit out.

She made me promise to get them speaking again if I wanted her help. Honestly, I didn't wanna get in it either. Unfortunately, I needed her assistance to make all of this possible.

"Oh my God Ryan." Two people walked out with a sign that read, *High School Prom*. Outta all the talks we had, I could tell she regretted not attending hers. A few minutes later, the forty people I hired, came out dressed up and Khloe started crying. Once her dad came, it was a wrap. She had waterworks coming down her face.

"Will you dance with me?" I asked and she turned beet red. I kissed her hand and pulled her in the middle of the floor.

"Ryan." I wiped the few tears that fell.

"Just enjoy it."

She and I danced a few songs before we sat down to eat. I pulled her chair out, handed her the roses and kissed the side of her neck. I nodded for everyone to sit as well. They had a buffet dinner, while we had the chef make whatever she wanted. The two of us had steak, mashed potatoes, green beans and corn on the cob. Yea, it's definitely not a meal the prom gives you. I turned her around to look at me.

Her dad stood and walked away. He knew I wanted to speak with her about my behavior towards her and gave us a minute. I didn't wanna do it here but I wanted to get everything out now to make sure when she received her other surprise it was done and never brought up again.

"Khloe, let me start by saying, I apologize from the bottom of my heart for disrespecting, embarrassing, treating you like shit and hiding you."

"Ryan." I shushed her with my index finger.

"I never pictured myself with a woman who wasn't skinny or even a model type." I had to be careful with my words. I wasn't sure if she'd smack me for using the word fat, BBW or chunky like Waleed used with Luna.

"I thought a man like me needed a trophy wife on my side to keep up an image." She rolled her eyes.

"That is until I met you and I don't mean it in a bad way, or referencing your weight." I took her hand in mine.

"Your confidence in your appearance, impressed the hell outta me and I think it's what made me fall for you." I noticed a smile forming on her lips.

"The way you carried yourself, your style of dress, you made your own money and even though you were in love with me, you refused to allow me to step all over you. You demanded my respect and K, on everything I love, you have it and all of my attention. No woman out here can get me to do any of this for them." I waved my hand at the setup I had done for her.

"I will say when you slept with that punk, I had every intention of ending your life." She gasped and her mouth dropped.

"But when you came to my house and I saw you, regardless of those hickeys, my heart was still beating for you and only you." I wiped her tears with my thumb.

"Khloe, you may have taken me back but I promise to continue making up for the dumb shit I put you through. I won't ever disrespect you again." She leaned in and we engaged in a deep and erotic kiss. I was ready to go to the room but I had a few more surprises for her. I stood her up and had her walk close to the edge but not too much because I know she's afraid of heights.

"Baby, this was beautiful. Thank you so much for tonight and what you just said." She pecked my lips and turned when she heard a noise.

"Look." I pointed in the dark sky and fireworks went off. I stood behind her and wrapped my arms around her waist as everyone enjoyed the ten-minute display.

"You ready for the rest?" She turned around.

"Ryan, this is enough."

"Not yet. Let's go." She kissed her father goodnight and extended her thanks to the staff and hired people, who helped with the prom affect. Most of them were employees from the hotel and their spouses.

We walked down the hall to the penthouse suite and she broke down again once she stepped inside. I had red and black balloons covering the entire ceiling. Rose petals were on the floor and four huge chocolate covered strawberry packages from edible arrangements was spread throughout the room.

Soft music was playing and of course candles were lit. Every light in the room was red and I asked the manager to place a canopy over the bed, which is upstairs. I was tryna remake her room where we first made love to one another. I made my way up the steps with her behind me. I had the edible massage oil on the bed and one of those toys she likes. Hell no, I didn't go in the store to get it. Luna did.

"Come here." I removed my tie and tossed the suit jacket on the floor.

"Did you like your surprise?" I swung her body around and unzipped the dress from behind.

"I love it." I placed a kiss on her shoulder blade and then her neck. My hands went under the straps and the dress fell to the ground. She wore no panties, which was my idea. I knew they'd be wet and I'd rather her juices slide down her leg so I can lick them up.

"Damn you sexy." Her head fell back on my chest.

"So are you," I felt her hand on my head and my lips found hers.

"Hold that thought." I took my shirt, shoes and pants off, grabbed the massage oil and squirted some on my hands. I let them rub all over and each time she moaned from my touch, my dick grew harder.

"You forgive me Khloe?" My hands were in between her legs as she stared down at me. I wouldn't let her sit or lie in the bed and it was killing her.

"Yes baby. I did the night you brought me home from the club. Sssssss." My tongue glided over her swollen clit.

"Can I do whatever I want to you tonight?"

"My body, is your body. Ahhhh fuck Ryan." I let two fingers go in and she came instantly.

"Stay right there." I picked my phone up and played the song I wanted her to hear. It was synced to the beats pill I had so it drowned out Pandora.

Just, Jusssssst, Just, Jusssssssssst, Let meee, make love to ya baby. I won't hurt, I won't hurt, I'll treat you ever so gentle, I'll make every little thing alright, honey you'll never forget this night, just let me make love to you baby.

229

I saw the smile on her face as the song by the O'Jays blasted through the speaker. She loved old school music and since this is what I wanna do, it only made sense to play it at this very moment. She laid back on the bed, opened her legs, picked the toy up and started to play with herself.

"How's it feel K?" I replaced her hand with mine and watched her fuck this thing. When her clit started to swell, I removed it, lifted her legs on my shoulder and penetrated her slow. I started making love to her and made her keep those eyes open.

"Are you gonna have my baby?"

"Yessssssss. Oh God yes." I could feel her juices spitting out and onto me.

"I love you Khloe Banks."

"I love you too Ryan Wells."

"Will you marry me?" She pushed on my chest to stop me.

"Don't play with me."

230

"I know it's only been less than a year that we've known one another but K, you are the only woman I want." I put her legs down, pulled out and picked my pants up. I planned on asking her at dinner but didn't wanna take away the prom moment.

"Oh my God." She covered her mouth and let the tears fall when I opened the velvet box.

"We don't have to get married tomorrow or even next year but I wanna show and prove, I want you in my life forever. Will you do me the honor and be my wife?" She shook her head yes over and over.

"You sure?"

"Boy, put my ring on." She held her hand out as I placed the ten-carat pear shaped diamond I got from Tiffany's on her finger.

"This is beautiful. I love you so much baby." She wrapped her arms around my neck.

"I promise to be a good role model and stepmother to Raina. And a good, loyal and faithful wife to you."

"I know you will, which is why you have this." I lifted her hand.

"Lay back baby." She pushed me down on the bed.

"For?"

"Your fiancé is about to do bad things to you."

"Shit, you don't have to tell me twice. Do you ma." All I can say is my fiancé had me at a loss for words with the things she did. I ain't never giving her up. Now, I have to get her and Luna speaking again.

Khloe

"You knew daddy?" I asked him on the phone. After putting it down for my fiancé last night, I didn't wanna get outta bed. Unfortunately, my bladder wouldn't let me stay in like I wanted. I tried to go back to sleep but the excitement of being Ryan's fiancé kept me awake. It was after eleven so I called my father while he slept.

"Of course, I did. He was supposed to do it during the prom thing so I could witness it."

"I'm sorry daddy. He told me that he didn't wanna spoil my prom moment."

"It's ok. As long as you're happy, nothing else matters. You are happy, aren't you?"

"I am dad. The things he said to me at the table were special and I honestly felt like he meant every word."

"He did."

"How do you know?"

"Because he came to the house a few days before and asked for your hand in marriage."

"Wow!"

"What? That's how a real man does it." I smiled because my father is very old fashioned.

"It's safe to say your mom may not attend."

"Oh well. Add her to the list." I shrugged my shoulders even though he couldn't see me.

"You're still not speaking to Luna?"

"Nope and believe it or not, I'm ok."

"I would feel the same way Khloe. But you do know she's sorry."

"I don't wanna talk about it. Are you coming by later?" I was making him dinner since he claims my mother is upset with him for not checking on her after what I did. Then he never had her back about Ryan yelling at her either. Therefore; she told him he won't get another meal outta her. And being a daddy's girl, I'm not letting him starve so of course I offered to make him dinner every night.

"Hell no."

"Daddy!"

"You outta your damn mind if I'm coming over and the two of you are still celebrating. I do not wanna hear it. Thanks, but no thanks." I busted out laughing.

"Fine. I'll call when we're home." After we hung up, I ordered room service with a little bit of everything. Ryan, may be skinny but he ate like a man who weighed three hundred pounds.

I knew it would be a while before the food came so I hopped in the shower and threw a robe on. I didn't have any other clothes besides the ones from last night.

"Thank you." I told the guy who brought a cart of food up. I handed him a tip outta Ryan's pocket and closed the door.

"Baby, come eat." I moved the covers off and placed kisses down his back.

"Eat what?"

"Food, nasty."

"I'll pass."

"Ryan, get up and eat. I wanna go sightseeing but my clothes are home." He rolled over and stared at me.

"Acting like a spoiled brat already and we're not even married yet." I smirked.

"You have clothes in the closet." He pointed and stood up.

"Stop staring at my dick."

"Why?" I folded my arms.

"Because you wanna go out and sight see, which means you're not giving me pussy."

"Now who's being spoiled?"

"Damn right. After last night, Ima want it like that every time." I started laughing as he made his way in the bathroom. I did any and everything to him under the sun and I'd do it all over again if he wants.

"You have to work for that." I stood in the bathroom watching him start the shower.

"That ring and this good ass dick is enough."

"I can admit that it's worth the soreness."

"That's it?" He pulled me close, untied my robe and had me step in.

"Well."

"Well what?" His hand squeezed my ass as he lifted me up and plunged inside.

"Well it's about to be even more sore." He wasn't lying. Ryan fucked me so good in the shower, I wanted to stay in the bed for the rest of the day. Of course, he didn't let me since I woke him up.

****

"K, let me talk to you for a minute?" Ryan said when he came in the house. We ended up spending the entire weekend in the hotel.

"Hello to you too." He kissed my lips and looked over my shoulder to see what I was cooking.

"Hi daddy." Raina came walking in when he stuck his hand under my shirt.

"Oh, hey! How was school?"

"Fine. When are we moving in the new house?" They finally found a six-bedroom house she liked and couldn't wait to move in.

"Whenever my fiancé says she's ready." He looked at me and Raina folded her arms against her chest.

237

"Ryan you never asked me."

"That's what I was coming to do now."

"Why would he ask you Ms. K? You're about to be his wife, and my stepmom. He's not going to let you stay here." She rolled her eyes looking around my house.

"Ugh ahh, heffa. Don't come for my house." She busted out laughing and I started making their plates. Once we all sat down to eat, I saw both of them staring at me and dropped my fork.

"What?"

"Welllllllll Ms. K." She refused to call me Khloe, no matter how many times I asked.

"Spit it out Raina." Ryan was shaking his head.

"Before you say anything let me finish." I placed my hands under my chin and stared at her. Something was up and the two of them were in on it.

"Ok. Am I gonna be mad." She shrugged her shoulders.

"Ok, I'm just gonna say it. Luna is sorry and she keeps begging everyone to get you to speak to her and quite frankly, I'm tired of her calling and texting me. I'm twelve and I think she forgets because she surely tells me off if I don't answer her calls or texts." I busted out laughing because Luna is a mess and I could see her doing exactly what Raina said.

"And, she told me if none of us can get you to talk to her, we're not invited to her wedding or to see my little cousin when he's born."

"Really! She said that?"

"And I thought your mother was petty." She started eating again. I looked at Ryan who was pretending he knew nothing.

"What?" He said and lifted his drink.

"What did she say to you because if she's threatening Raina, I know for a fact she did it to you too."

"You know better than that." He gave me a crazy look. Luna fucked around and played with him a lot but the times he was serious, she knew to leave him alone.

"I asked her to help me get the things ready for your surprise an she only did it because I promised to get you to talk to her."

"RYAN!"

"Don't Ryan me. I didn't know what type of jewelry you liked. The size of your clothes and shoes. She had to help." He shrugged his shoulders.

"Why didn't I have underclothes then." I waited for him to answer.

"That was to benefit me." He leaned in and kissed on my neck.

"Oh my God, y'all are gonna make me sick. Can I eat upstairs or in a different room?"

"Girl, be quiet." Ryan mushed her in the head.

"So, are you gonna speak to her?"

"I don't know. Right now, I'm happy and I don't want anyone to ruin it." I stood and went in the kitchen. I felt his presence behind me and turned. He was leaning on the door looking sexy as hell.

"I got your back for whatever you decide but don't let your pride make you miss out on more."

"That's easy for you to say. Your best friend told you." He came over.

"I get it K and its your decision. All I ask is you don't take it out on me tonight because I'm horny. Matter of fact, take that shit out on me in the bedroom." I smacked him on the arm.

"I love you K."

"I love you too. Do you think I should speak to her?"

"Not tonight. Stay mad and…" I stopped him from being nasty again.

"Go take a bath. Raina and I will clean up."

"Really!"

"Hell no. Raina, does though." I walked away cracking up. I turned around and he was biting down on his lip, staring at me. It only turned me on, more than I already was.

"When are we moving?"

"Whenever you want and no yo momma can't come over and she better not get a damn key." Again, he had me laughing. I went upstairs to take a nice hot bath and I can say, it relaxed me a lot. Now all I have to do is give my man some hot and steamy sex.

Lamar

"Grandma, my dad doesn't want me around uncle Lamar." I heard my niece say over the phone. My mom called to see her since it's been a while. She had her on speaker because I wanted to know why we hadn't seen her either.

"What do you mean Raina? He's your uncle and I'm your grandmother. Your mom would not approve of what he's doing?"

"Grandma, the woman who molested me, caught me at uncle Lamar's house. He was supposed to protect me from her but he wanted to be nasty with his dirty girlfriend and left me to fend for myself. She did bad things to me in that house." I felt like shit listening to her say that and my mom gave me the evilest look ever. She knew about the bitch Veronica bullying and touching my niece but she had no idea, I let the shit happen in my house. Thinking with my dick, allowed my niece to be violated and I was fucked up over it. I only found out because this is the hundredth time my mom tried to see Raina and she wasn't tryna come around me.

"I understand Raina but my house isn't the same."

"I know but he may pop up and I don't wanna see him."

"But your dad let it happen."

"NO HE DIDN'T. HE HAD NO IDEA WHAT SHE WAS DOING AND WHEN HE DID, SHE COULDN'T BE AROUND ME ANYMORE. AND STOP BRINGING UP MY MOM WOULD HAVE A FIT AND THAT MY DAD LET IT HAPPEN." Raina snapped and my mom was pissed.

"Little girl, don't talk to me like that. I am still the adult and…"

"Then act like it grandma and understand where I'm coming from. I'm not saying uncle Lamar would hurt me but you're tryna put me in a position to be around someone, I don't wanna be. Why can't you understand?" You could hear Raina crying and some noise in the background. Someone was asking her, if she were ok.

"Hello. Is anyone there?" The woman spoke and I had no idea who she was.

"Yea, why is my niece pretending like she doesn't wanna be around us? What y'all over there poisoning her with lies?" I was fed up at this point.

"I'll be right back Raina."

"But I don't wanna go over there." I heard my niece whining in the background. My mom asked who the woman was and I had no idea. It could be the chick Khloe, Risky was dealing with but then again, I heard he was with the therapist or some shit.

"And you're not. Give me a minute." You could hear a door close and the woman got back on the phone.

"Hi, who am I speaking to?"

"This is her uncle Lamar."

"Hi Lamar, this is Khloe, Ryan's fiancé." *His fiancé?* This nigga didn't even ask to marry my sister and he's about to tie the know with some fat bitch. Hell yea, I had a problem with it.

"Raina doesn't want to come over there but your mom is more than welcome to meet us somewhere or…" I cut her fat ass right off.

"Now you listen to me bitch."

"Bitch?"

"You heard me. My mom has her own house and don't need to meet her grandmother anywhere, but here. Second, who the fuck you think you are tryna dictate shit? I'm her uncle and if I wanna see her, then bring her the fuck over. Do I make myself clear?" I didn't hear anything.

"Hello?"

"I'm here. I was waiting for you to finish. Can I speak now?"

"Go the fuck head."

"First off motherfucker, don't ever think its ok to disrespect me, your niece or your sister."

"My sister? What the fuck you talking about?"

"The minute you allowed the stupid bitch to attack and violate your niece in yo pissy ass house, you disrespected her. All so you can get your little dick sucked by some dirty bitch.

Then you wanna call Raina all types of spoiled brats and a whiny bitch because she doesn't wanna be around you."

"What?"

"Oh, I've seen the nasty text messages you sent her because she doesn't wanna be around you. You and I both know, if her father saw these you wouldn't even be on this phone bitching like a chick. Last but not least, don't call this phone again telling her she better come see you or your mother because it ain't happening, captain."

"Bitch, you're not her mother."

"You're right but I'm gonna be her stepmother and no one is gonna bully, torture or make my daughter feel obligated to see them if she doesn't want to. You of all people should respect it after everything she's been through but you're so fucking selfish and tryna bully her into coming there. What would your sister say to you allowing her daughter to be attacked while she was in your care? Huh? How would she feel knowing you fucked the very same woman who did it? Or the fact you're tryna kill Raina's father over jealousy?" How the fuck did she know all that?

"Exactly! Stay silent motherfucker and don't dial this number again because if you do, I can promise you that Ryan, Waleed or even myself will put a fucking bullet in between your eyes now fuck with it, if you want." I looked down at the phone and noticed she hung up. I tried to call back but the number was blocked.

"What the hell is wrong with you Lamar? Did you sleep with the woman who dud those things to Raina? Are you trying to kill her father?"

"Ma, you don't understand."

"Jesus, please be a fence. My son is going to be buried right next to his sister." She stood up.

"Really!"

"Yes because you're going after a dangerous man. He will do anything for Raina and if that woman is indeed his fiancé, he will go to war for her. You know that because he was the same with your sister. Lamar, leave the state or something. Please, I can't lose another child." I stood there in shock listening to my own mother wish death on me and tell me to leave the state in the same breath. Why wasn't anyone listening to me about Risky being the one who got her killed? Do I have to spell it out? Matter of fact, I'm gonna do one better and make that nigga wish he never knew me or my sister.

****

Its been a little over a week since the Khloe bitch talked all that bullshit and hung up on me but I was still mad. Who the hell did she think she was, tryna tell me right from wrong? If my memory serves me correctly that punk nigga, still fucked Veronica after she made her throw up too. She had some nerve tryna call me out when her damn man ain't shit. I know that because I'm sitting outside the doctor's office snapping pictures of him hugging some other bitch. Nigga got a whole fiancé at home and he still fishing.

"Hello." I answered the call from the dude who was about to be my new boss and allow me to run shit.

"Meet me at the address I'm sending to your phone in fifteen minutes."

"Got it." I snapped a few more photos and the best one was of the chick placing her lips on his. I couldn't wait to show the stuck-up bitch, this one.

I drove to the spot he told me to meet him at, which was a damn strip mall. There weren't a lotta people there but it wouldn't be since damn near everything was closed, except the pharmacy. I was about to send him a text asking where he was when this chick stepped out this nice ass truck. I waited to see what she would do and once she went in the pharmacy, I followed. You could hear her asking for some Robotusssin and a few other over the counter medicines. One of them must be sick and right now I don't care who because she and I, are about to have some fun. She grabbed the bag from the lady and walked out the door, with my creepy ass right behind her.

"What up bitch? Talk that shit now." She turned around with no facial expression.

"Well, well, well. We meet again, I see." I was shocked she remembered me.

"You damn right, now you're gonna take a ride with me."

"The hell I am. My man is at home waiting for me and."

"Actual facts you're lying." She folded her arms across her chest.

"Oh yea. How the fuck you know?"

"Because I just left him with his other bitch." I pulled my phone out and showed her all the photos of her nigga hugged up.

"Yea, look at the time and date. Ain't no need to lie. Yo nigga is as grimy as the rest of us." I could see how watery her eyes got.

"Get in the car." I pointed to my ride.

"No." She moved past me.

"GET IN THE FUCKING CAR!" I shouted and put my gun on the side of her waist. She walked over to it and I heard someone call my name. I couldn't make out the voice.

"Hello, Khloe." Her eyes got real big.

"I think the three of us should take a ride. What you think Lamar?" He said and I didn't say a word. I made my way to the black suburban waiting on the other side of the parking lot. Who is this nigga and what type of shit Khloe got going

on?

Julie

"Yo, you pregnant yet?" Oscar asked and picked the test up. I took tissue off the roll and wiped myself.

"You tell me since the test is in your hand."

WHAP! My face turned sideways from the force his hand caused.

"What I tell you about talking shit?" I wiped the blood off my lip.

"And you promised my sister would be dead by now but we can't always get what we want."

Hell yea, I'm sleeping with the exact nigga who's supposed to marry my sister. A man like Oscar needs a ride or die, beautiful and loyal chick by his side. Luna is nothing of the sort. She's fat, thinks her shit don't stink and after putting me in the hospital some years ago, I'm gonna make sure to return the favor. The only difference is her hospital visit will be to the morgue.

I'm sure her fat ass told the story of how we're related but let me reiterate it a little. Evidently, my mom was a ho and sleeping with a taken man. I say evidently because she was dead before I was old enough to ask questions. Anyway, she popped up pregnant, had the baby and supposedly tried to use me as a pawn in getting him back.

Luna's mom found out and left him. He was devastated and spent tons of money, countless hours of tryna make it up and even terminated my mom, in order to get her to come home. His wife, my stepmom sat me down and explained it to me one day but I still blamed her. Had she not left him, my mother would still be here. She tried to tell me my mom made many attempts on her life but I didn't believe it. Like I said, I was too young to know anything and since she's not here to defend herself, I can think what I want.

Now the way Oscar and I met is because after leaving the ICU unit Luna put me in, I ran off to Mexico to hide. I was scared my father would find and kill me. For the first two years, I got a job and since the pay is so low, I had to stay in homeless shelters because I couldn't afford anywhere to live. I

253

met some chick in the store who took pity on me and introduced me to the stripping life.

Fortunately for me, Oscar owned it. The first day we met, he asked if I were a virgin because the men there, may or may not want sex. Once I told him yes, he never allowed me to strip. I had to be a bottle girl and ended up his woman.

We have two kids together but they came a couple of years ago. We had to keep them a secret because of the stupid ass agreement between him and my sister.

If you're wondering how I was able to be with Waleed, it's because I caught Oscar cheating and left him. I moved back to Jersey because I figured enough time passed and my father wouldn't be looking for me. I met Waleed at a club up north and the two of us hooked up. I figured Oscar was doing his thing so why not do me?

Waleed and I stayed together for a while, I got pregnant and terminated it. Oscar said, I'd never have kids with another man and begged me to come home, which is why I left. But not before sleeping with Lamar to piss him off. Waleed can say he didn't cheat all he wants but a woman knows when her man steps out. I didn't care how hurt he was because my real man wanted me home and I went running.

Now we're sitting here waiting on the results of a pregnancy test. I grabbed his hand and glanced at the test. When I looked up he was smiling.

"Now let's go put our plan in motion. I'm tired of waiting." He stepped out and I followed.

"Oscar?" He turned to look at me.

"Damn, you sexy. Can I get some before we go?" I asked.

"I don't know, can you?" He smirked and pulled the back of my hair and had me staring in his face.

"You do know it's gonna be a war?"

"I do."

"Who you riding for?"

"My man. What you think this is?" The two of us fucked the hell outta one another and got ready to get rid of my sister and allow him to take his seat on the throne.

****

"When she comes out Julie don't get stupid." Oscar said as we waited for Luna to emerge from the mall. It was Saturday and packed like crazy, which made it even better because no one would be paying us any mind.

"I got it Oscar. I'm not an amateur."

"Not in bed, that's for sure." I turned and kissed his lips.

"She's on her way out boss." One of the guys spoke in the walkie talkie.

"Its time."

I hopped out the car and hurried to the door, she supposedly was coming out of and ran straight into her. She pushed the shit outta me and two big ass men came outta nowhere. We were prepared for her bodyguards so when their bodies hit the ground, Luna appeared to be afraid and that's exactly the way I wanted it. People were running and yelling but no one stopped to ask if either of us needed help.

"What the fuck you want Julie?" I saw her text on the phone and then place it in her back pocket. Not knowing if it was Waleed or not I had to hurry up. She started speed walking in the parking lot, which pissed me off because I had heels on. I pulled her arm and she stopped.

"I just wanna know if you're gonna be a good stepmother to my child?"

"WHAT?"

"Yea bitch. Me and Waleed are expecting."

"What up Luna?" Oscar said and it looked like all the blood drained from her face. I mean, she was scared to death for some reason.

"Oscar, whattt... what... are you doing here?"

"I came to shop but who knew I'd run into you? Are you ok? You look pale."

"Ummm. No, I'm fine." She was still stuttering. And once she tried to move past, the bags in front of her fell and I now knew why she was scared.

CLICK! Oscar had his gun out.

"You better tell me you're fucking bloated because by the size of your stomach, I'd say you were pregnant." He snatched her by the hair, placed the gun under her chin and asked again.

"Oscar please." She had tears racing down her face.

"Did you get married?" I asked lifting her hand up, after seeing that huge ass rock on her finger. Oscar's entire demeanor changed and I swore the devil himself came out.

"Bitch! Are you married?" He asked and in a matter of five seconds everything went from sugar to shit.

TO BE

CONTINUED...

Please remember that even though this book is fiction, there are people who are going through this every day. Just because you, someone you know, a family member and etc... aren't dealing with these type of issues, please don't assume its not happening. What you may go through, isn't always what someone else is. What you allow, isn't the same as what someone else will allow. Don't make assumptions when you don't know what's really going on.

If this book series has touched one person, then I did my job and I hope they become stronger and get through whatever it is, they may be going through. We are living in different times and everything isn't always what it seems.

If you or anyone you know has been bullied, or contemplating suicide please talk to someone. You can also contact the suicide hotline. Some may know it and others may not. I listed it down below in case someone needs them.

National Suicide Prevention Hotline

(There is also an online chat if you don't want to speak to

someone directly)

1-800-273-8255

Cyber bully Hotline

1-800-420-1479

National Center For Missing and Exploited Children Cyber Tipline

1-800-843-5678

These are just some phone numbers. If you search online, there are a whole lot more.

CPSIA information can be obtained
at www.ICGtesting.com
Printed in the USA
LVHW011657180119
604419LV00014B/593/P